MURDER INC.

Gutter Publications
1461 a 1st ave ste 234
New York, NY 10021
guttermag.com

1

Entering that candy store that cold day in October turned out to be the worst day in my life. It was the beginning to the end for me. Everything about that day was all wrong. It was raining like cats and dogs and the wind was blowing like no other. I had on a cheap ass windbreaker that had holes in it and a pair of button down tailored jeans. My soul was telling me from jump that I should not get involved with Tracey and polo. Both of them were seasoned criminals with no family and no sense of direction in life. Polos' mother had abandoned him way before he could spell his own name and Tracey's' mother went blind from drinking so much; Actually I don't know what she went blind from but she drank so much that that would be the logical answer. They had been planning this robbery for weeks unbeknownst to me. I was the only sucker in all of this. The plan was to rob the store during lunch break and be back in school before the lunch bell sounded. They thought that would be the perfect alibi. I just happen to see those fools third period on my way to gym and they asked me if I wanted to get down with them on a paper chase. Trying to be down I agreed and was told to meet them in the back of the school during lunch break. Both of them were well prepared decked out in black army fatigues and dark hoodies. During fourth period, my stomach begins to churn inside. I knew both of these fools all of my life and I knew what they were about, trouble. We all came out of the same projects, Lincoln houses, in Harlem. It is a world unto itself where cats eat dogs and little twelve year olds are doing B& E's on a regular. Coming from Lincoln you are crowned into the life of crime whether you like it or not. It is a sin in my community to even dream of leaving the hood. As the lunch bell rang out over the P.A.

system, a cold sweat began to overtake my body like the aids virus. My clothes became soaked with salt water as I exited my classroom door to make my entrance into a life of crime by heading for the back of the school. Everything seemed to be moving in slow motion and the corridor to the back door became a blur in front of me. It seemed like I would never get there, deep inside I didn't want to get there but I knew I would be called a punk if I didn't and to me that was worst than committing the crime. As I opened, the door to the back of the school Tracey and polo were standing there like hawks waiting to devour their next meal. I was ushered to the kiddy park directly across from the school and given a little black pistol that I later learned to be a twenty-five. I summoned all of the courage within me to ask" why do I have to be the one to carry the gun?" without hesitation Tracey replied, " because me and polo did this a million times already, if you want to be down than you are going to have to prove it." yea right! I didn't really want to be down anyway, but I was afraid of saying no, so I went along with the program. It is not as if I was afraid of Tracey and polo, I just did not want to be known as soft for not doing it. I took the gun and tucked it safely in my Jan sport book bag between my history book and my gym shorts. We began walking at a fast pace to our destination to the corner store on 125th street and Amsterdam. It was only three blocks from the school but they wanted to get in and get out so that the end of lunch would find us back on our way to class where we should be. Tracey gave me a pep talk before we entered the store. "Me and polo is going to come in right after you, just go act like you are going to buy something and when you get to the register pull out on his ass and make him give you the money". "What do I say; I replied in a soft tone of voice" polo cuts in. "you say whatever it is you have to say to get that mother fucker to give you the money". Shaking uncontrollably, I open the door and enter the bodega. I head for the back to the soda box and pull down a yoo-hoo from the top shelf. The bottle is pressed cold against my sweaty palm as I make my way to the cash register. In an authoritative voice that commands attention the cashier asserts," that's fifty cents for the drink, are you buying the cookies too?' holding the cookies as if hesitant to purchase them I respond," yeah, uhm, ring them up too". "That'll be ninety-five cents total young man." I go into my bag to pull out a piece of currency as if to pay for the items. I hand him a dollar bill while simultaneously pulling out the pistol with my right hand dropping the bag in front of me. "Give me my change and some you spick mother fucker and hurry the fuck up." I didn't know I had all of that base in my voice; I was really getting into the role as a seasoned stick up kid. I wasn't fooling myself though, I was pissing all over myself; literally. The cashier was scared to death as well and his fear was evident, all I could hear was him saying," oh, my God! Don't kill me! Please God don't kill me...." the cashier is so nervous it is taking what appears to be a long time. My nerves are rattled, so much so I don't even notice the fact that Tracey and polo are doing nothing to help me, in fact, they are not even acting like they are a part of the whole thing. I cocked the pistol and it starts to shake in my hand from my fear. My heart begins to palpitate uncontrollably. I begin to get somewhat disoriented and dizzy for a brief second. In that blink of an eye, a shot from the pistol rings out. The bullet finds a home in the cashiers' chest cavity. I apparently squeezed the trigger in my nervousness. The impact of the bullet sends the cashiers' body slamming into the shelves behind him, than slumping to the floor lifeless. I look over the counter in disbelief; I thought there were no bullets in the gun. "Oh shit! I didn't mean to shoot you; man...I didn't mean to shoot you". I wait for a response from the lifeless body as if I was going to get one. Reality that I had just killed a man had set in, what was I going to do now. I look around and polo and Tracey are nowhere to be found, they had abandoned me. Turns out, they were not as real as I thought they were. I decided I was going all the way from that point on, if I had a body I was dam sure going to get what I came in there for. I jumped over the counter and grabbed the dollar bill out of the cashiers' bloody hands and the remaining bills from out of the register. I jumped back over to retrieve my book bag, I didn't realize than but I would soon discover my bus pass and I.D. had slipped out of the bag. I head for the door and run out like a bat out of hell running up 125th street towards morning Side Avenue. While doing the hundred-yard dash up the block I could see the number thirty-three bus on its way up the block coming from Broadway. I cross over to the eastbound side of 125th street so that I could catch the bus on the corner of 125th street opposite the st. Mary catholic church on the corner of morning side by the southern fried chicken spot. As the bus approaches I begin to wipe the blood from my hands I dig into my bag for my bus pass and to my amazement it was gone. By than I could see and hear police cars at the far corner of the next block on Amsterdam at the scene of the crime. For some reason, even though I had the money to get on the bus or even take a cab for that matter, I decided I was going to walk. I guess when your adrenaline is rushing and you are scared to death you can't think straight. I walk down two blocks and turned on to Eighth Avenue on my way uptown cutting through st Nicholas projects. I wiped the gun down and threw it in a garbage can by the basketball courts on seventh as I was exiting the projects. By than the rain had given me a bath and I was completely clean of red impurities from the cashiers' chest wounds. I made a pit stop at the mc Donald's on 132nd st and Lenox Avenue before going home. I ordered a cheeseburger and fries and a chocolate shake, I guess that replaced the yoo-hoo that I had dropped in the store; one way or another I was going to enjoy a chocolate drink. The bills were soiled with blood as I handed them to the mc Donald's cashier. I begin to see flashes of that guy lying on the floor as I passed her the money for my burger, fries and shake. She looked at me suspiciously, as I left with my goods; I guess I would to if someone just gave me some money with blood all over it. I turned the corner in a hurried fashion walking down the block on 132nd st pass the old fire station and the Lenox terrace. When I got to the corner there were niggers hanging inside of Maxwell's donut shop playing tempest and Pac-man. I stopped for a minute to talk to my man mighty mouse from the other side of the projects and than went upstairs. When I got there, my mother was in her room on the phone running her jibbers with her church friends and my sister debra was in the living room watching fraggle rock on HBO. I headed for the room to count the rest of my dough. It didn't take but a second to count all of seventy-three dollars. Can you believe this shit; I had just killed a man for seventy-three dollars. If I had to split it with polo and Tracey, I would have been fucked up. Shit there was no way I was giving them shit. Not only did they leave me, but they didn't even act like they were down with me. The anger in me made me forget about how tough I thought they were. I was the toughest nigger at that point because I had gone all the way with it. I feared being called a punk by two punks. It is always like that. True soldiers will always be the one that you least expect it from.

Laying down on my bed in a trance, I am running over the events that just took place a couple of hours ago when I hear a knock on my bedroom door. The knock startled me at first but it was followed by my mothers' voice." Shaheem, go get the phone in the living room, Stephanie is on the phone. Tell her you will call her back, I got Sister Gray on the other line". I go to get the phone in the living room; there was slob all over the phone from someone drooling all over it. I know it was either my mother or my stepfather; they both have a habit of that. You can taste the saliva from their mouths and smell their funky breaths all over the phone if you don't wipe it down with your shirt or something. "Hello, who is this?" I asked in a voice that commanded attention. "It's me bam bam, what happened to you today mister? I immediately get on the defensive and am alarmed that she knew what I had just done. What do you mean what happened to me, who told you something happened to me and why are you running your mouth like that?" " you said you was going to wait for me after school, Sabrina said she saw you , Tracey and polo at lunch time and neither one of y'all assess came back to school after lunch period; what's up with that?" for a minute there I thought she had me. I thought my cover was blown for sure. In the streets if one person knows you did something than you can pretty much call it a wrap, your as good as busted. I could hear my mother in the other room," boy get off the phone, I told you somebody was on the other line" okay, I'm getting off now". I told bam of my mothers one minute warning to get off. "Bam I have to get off the phone, I exclaimed in a hurried voice". "Well I just called to tell you that they killed that Dominican man that owned that store on the corner, it was stupid police out there when I came home". This prompted me to click the other line to make a special request of sister gray. "Bam, hold on for a second". I clicked the other line to discover sister gray had already hung up anyway. I informed my mother of the news but added my little twist so that she would not try to call her write back and make me get off the phone. "Ma, sister gray said she will call you back in a little while, she said she had to run out to the supermarket before it closed". She quickly replied in her manly like voice, "that still doesn't mean for you to stay on the phone all night." Yea, yea I know". I quickly click back, "bam, bam you still there?" "Yea, I'm right hear she retorted in her smooth sexy voice". "Anyway let me finish telling you what happened. Whoever did it had a beef with him or something. They shot his ass in the heart. It was probably the mob or something, my mamma plays her numbers in there all the time, they say he don't like to pay when you win; at least that's what my mamma and them say". My mind takes a breather, they don't know who killed him, or do they? What does bam really know, she's no Shirley Holmes. I might just be home free, no use in worrying about it now anyway, what is done is done.

"Well bam I gotta go before my moms start breaking. I'll see you in school tomorrow." There was a silence on the phone for a half a second. "Aight than, she replied, call me later if you can" the phone went straight to the dial tone before I could get another word out. She must have been pissed I was getting off the phone so quickly. Normally we would be on the phone all night, sometimes sleeping with the phone in our hands or off the hook on the floor. After I hung up the phone I went to the bathroom to take a leak and than to my room to lay down, I was kinda tired and rightfully so; the life that was drained out of the store owner was drained out of me. To my amazement, I wasn't thinking about the events that took place a couple of hours ago. I guess I was still into my new role as a killer and stick up kid. Not a moment had passed into that thought that I began to doze off. I was ushered into slumber with both Tracey and polo on my mind. I carried their images with me to sleep and I began to dream of our individual child hoods.

2

They say you only dream a total of eleven minutes during your sleeping hours; this dream seems to be taking days, months and years to wrap itself up. I am dreaming about the good times we use to have as kids even though we were poor as hell. My dreams would reveal I was just as bad as polo and Tracey were. We would go down to the tip of central park on 111th street and wait for white boys to ride their bikes by the central park pool. One of us would jump in front of a young bike rider while the others would jump out of the bushes pushing the rider off the bike. We would do this until all of us had enough bikes to ride uptown. I must admit we had so much fun. When we were not   robbing white boys, we were breaking day on the weekends in the hallways of one of the big buildings in our projects. The halls were always filled with zombies, well not exactly zombies. Crack heads to be more precise. In all of the madness of growing up in a poverty-stricken environment poor black folks always know how to make light of a bad situation. As kids, we know that we are poor but only in relation to people around us telling us that we are poor. We know we don't have shit but we make due and keep it moving. Where little white boys in girls found pleasure riding bikes through central park and going to ballet lessons, little black kids enjoyed jumping on pissy mattresses in vacant lots and playing at the fire hydrant in the summer time. We enjoyed taking train rides to nowhere, playing stickball with a broomstick, and running up and down infested project corridors.

"Knock, knock, knock", am I still dreaming or is that a knock on the door? The knock on the door wakes me from my dream of my youth and I am transported back to reality. My little sister runs to the door, "who is it', she asks in a soft child like voice? A commanding manly voice replies, "its detective harts field, is your mother home?" that was all I needed to hear to get my ass on my feet. I silently stand by my bedroom door waiting for my mother to go to the door to answer it. The fear that I had not felt was slowly overtaking my body. As my mother walked from the hallway from her room to the door I could see my life flash right before me. I knew the moment she opened that door my life would change forever. As she approached the door she asks once again as if she did-n't hear my sister, "who is it?" the same response was given," this is detective hartsfield from the 19th precinct, can I have a moment of your time maam." My mother opens the door with confidence that this is not a hoax or some deranged lunatic posing as a cop. "what is going on my mother asks, is my hus-band alright?" "Husband maam, I am not here concerning your husband. Do you have a son by the name of shaheem Thomas?" my mother was taken aback by the mere mention of my name. "Yes I have a son name shaheem; my boy isn't in any kind of trouble is he?" "I don't know yet", detective hart-field replied, "There was a robbery homicide at a local store on the Westside this afternoon and we found this." He shows her a bus pass that is obviously mine. "Is he in, I need to speak with him to see if he could possibly help us in getting to the bottom of what happened today." "Shaheem! In a loud voice, get out here." I assure you officer..., what did you say your name was again? He interjects,"hartfield maam. "Well Mr. Hartfield my boy don't know nothing bout no robbery homo-cide."

When I got to the door and saw that officers face I knew deep inside I was going down; I also knew deep down inside I was going down for a long time. "Shaheem did you go to school today, my mother asked in an angry voice?" "Yes mamma, I went to school, what you ask me that for?" "Never you mind, were you in school all day?" I hesitate with my response," yes'. "well you see there Mr. Officer my boy was in school all day now if you will excuse me", she tries to close the door" the officer places his foot between the door simultaneously pulling out my bus pass from his trench coat pocket. "Can you explain to your mother why I have your bus pass in my possession?" I give a puzzled look trying to come up with a lie before my face gives me away. "No, I don't know how you got it." "Than how did you get home?" "I walked, I responded in a semi confidant voice." "I am going to have to ask you and your son to come across town with me to the station house." "For what", my mother asks? "It is apparent your son was at the least at the scene of the crime and for that alone I believe he might be instrumental in solving the case." My mother dashes to her bedroom to get clothing and her pocket book. She calls our neighbor from the fifth floor to come upstairs and mind my sister. As officer hartfield and I wait for my neighbor to come upstairs, he is looking at me as if he was looking into my very soul. My mother returns to the door. Just as she returned, I could see charmayne, our neighbor coming up the stairs from the fifth floor. " thanks so much for doing this for me girl", my mother says in a hurried type of voice," I'll be back as soon as I can, I'll tell you all about it when I get back." "You go right ahead, charmayne responds, I got this". My mother presses for the elevator. The elevator comes and I am shuttled from the elevator to an awaiting detective car parked right in front of the building. I was not handcuffed; I didn't know what to think at this point. Little did I know that was the last time I would taste freedom for years to come. The drive way across town in the back of that police car was the longest drive I ever took. Every light seem to stay at red and every block seem to be longer than the days in a week. My mother seem to be mumbling all the way there. I could not make out exactly what she was saying. I'd like to think it was a cross between shock and anger all at the same time. We finally arrived in front of the twenty-ninth precinct. I was taken to the interrogation room on the second floor. The room had no windows and the brick walls felt like solid ice when my skin pressed up against it. There were three aluminum chairs; two of them had broken handles and a long wooden bench that had names of former occupants burned into the wood. I can tell by the names on the wood that they all were crazy. There was sinister and Allah born, murder mike, deadeye, homicide, Jack Frost, and David two guns. Officer Hartsfield asked my mother if she would mind waiting outside in the hallway while he and his partner talked to me. He told him it was routine and that it would not take long. He also told her if I cooperated, I could be out in no time. That statement persuaded my mother to allow them to interrogate me without her being present. To her they just wanted to talk to me about my identification being at the scene of the crime. That was no biggie to her, after all, kids lose things. His partner came in and he appeared to be a hard ass. All the while, I was trying to think of something to say that would get me off the hook. His partner took a seat next to me and introduced himself. "Hey there son, my name is detective davis." I responded with a nod of affirmation of his name and authority. " my partner and I are here to not only get to the bottom of the situation that took place today, we are also here to see if we can come up with a solution to your problem." "What problem, I asked?" "You see son, we know you were in the store and we know you did it. What we don't know is why you did it and if in fact you acted alone. Now you can make it light on yourself or we can come down on you like a ton of bricks, take your pick." He now had my undivided attention. My nerves were rattled. Not only did he know, but he was going to make sure I got the business if I didn't cooperate. What could I say that would possibly help me out at this point? I was ready to give a full confession right then and there but something was prodding me to hold out a little bit longer. Detective hartsfield adds his two cents in. " it would kill your mother to know that her son is going to go to jail for the rest of his life, you've never been to so much as a precinct before now son, your record is as clean as a whistle." "You give us a signed confession and we will see to it that the judge gives you the maximum amount of leniency allowable by the law". "So what's it going to be, detective Saxon asks?" I was mentally exhausted at this point, I just wanted to go home, or at least somewhere, where I could just lie down. "What if I was guilty with an explanation?" "Now we are getting somewhere, guilty with an explanation is what we are looking for, remarked detective davis. I'm sure we could persuade the prosecutor to work something out, are you ready to talk?" "I think so, I replied". "Good, replied detective davis, I'll get a pad and a pencil and we will get out of your way and let you tell what happened in writing". He gets the pad, pen, and exit with detective hartsfield, leaving me alone with nothing but a pen, a pad, and my thoughts. At first, I was going to tell it like it was, I was going to take polo and Tracey down with me. For some reason I felt like that wouldn't help me any, in fact I thought it would hurt me. I opted to leave them out of the equation. I began to write bit by bit adding and subtracting truth and falsehood as I wrote. I did a mock up in my mind before I even committed it to paper. I decided the version I was going to tell was that I found the gun in the back of the school and that I decided to go into the store to scare the cashier as a prank. The gun went off and I was frightened and decided to make it look like I robbed the joint. Quite clever for a fifteen-year-old kid, I owed my savvy ness to growing up in my hood. I had seen jailbirds growing up who did things and were released in no time. My sense of time was lacking. I knew it couldn't be that bad in prison, after all, my father was in there and I would speak to him often on the phone at my grandmothers' house. He didn't seem to be sweating being in prison. Every time I spoke to him he would say that he would be home soon, how was I to know that be home soon to him meant in the next twenty-years. No sooner than I had finished writing both detectives came back in the room. Detective Davis grabs the pad I had written on and gives it a looking over. He pauses in thought over the finished product for what seemed like an eternity. In a soft jovial voice he says, "This has got to be the best bullshit I have seen in my twelve years on the force, but you know what, we are going to go with the bullshit because you didn't take us through the bullshit by totally trying to deny what you've done. There is something not right about it but we are going to leave it at that, look this over harts". Detective hartsfield looks it over and affirms the bullshit, "yea your right, that's some good bullshit alright. For someone that has never been in trouble a day in his life this shit looks like a professional confession if I ever saw one". They called my mom in and informed her that I had given them a written confession. She dammed near caught a heart attack right there. "Shaheem did you do what these officers say you did, did you kill somebody?" "I didn't mean to kill him mamma"! She began to cry profusely. They escorted my mother out of the room and told her that I would be booked and processed and that I would be downtown by morning or late evening tomorrow. After I gave my confession the police treated me like shit from than on out. They didn't intentionally treat me like shit, it was just in their nature to treat all criminals like shit and since I had given a confession, I was as guilty as any criminal found guilty in a court of law. My case was simple and airtight to them, shit a trial was out of the way; there was no need. I could only be at the mercy of the court from this point out; I was sure going to need it. This was also a lot of overtime for those two dick head detectives. After they formally booked and fingerprinted me, they took me downtown to central booking personally. Under normal circumstances I would have went on the blue NYPD cattle truck but it was late that night and the pick for the day had left, not to mention I was a juvenile. I was booked as an adult, which meant I would not be going to juvenile court at 440 Lafayette. I was going straight to 100-centre Street. The streets were as desolate as the desert that night. The ride to one police plaza felt like that was my last ride in a car forever. We drove down the FDR drive to get there and I was just imagining how things would look when I got out, that's if I ever got out. I was trying to remember as many landmarks as possible so that I could see how much things had changed when I got out. I knew that much because all of the older jail birds from my hood would always come home talking about how much the block had changed. For me it was always the same ole block, nothing ever changed, but for them it was a different ghetto altogether. By the time we got to one police plaza the bullpens was packed like sardines. There is nowhere to lay down because the floor is packed with dope fiends, derelicts, and just regular Joes' trying to get some sleep before the storm, a nigger wants to be alert when that time is handed down to their ass. The seats had metal barriers between them so that a nigger couldnt lay his ass across the motherfucker to sleep. I got there too late to get the bullpen special happy meal, which is nothing, more than cold tea with no sugar and a stale bologna sandwich with no condiments. I couldn't get any sleep if I wanted to, not only was niggers running their jibbers all night, you had counselors doing background checks on niggers to determine what they would tell the judge on your behalf. All they did was ask for an address where you could be reached if you made bail and was there anybody there to vouch for you. That made me think there was hope for me for a minute; just maybe I might make bail, shit who am I kidding, if I did get a bail my mother doesn't have two nickels to rub together to get me out. I was losing my mind thinking about what would happen. To add more stress was the fact that I could tell what time it was. In central booking there are no windows, everything remains the same constantly in there. I had no idea that I was standing all that time, it was morning and morning court was in process. A seat became available on the other side of the cell, I immediately made a dash for it to claim it as my own. A crack head was lying in front of where I would need to put my feet to sit there. "Pardon me duke", I asked in a humble voice. "My name aint duke, he moves his body as if he understands what I was trying to get at, go ahead rest yourself young blood." I must have been sitting down for less than a minute when the legal aid called my name. "Shaheem Thomas, is there a shaheem Thomas here?" I yell out from across the cell, "shaheem Thomas right here." "Hey Mr. Thomas, my name is Mr. stillman and I am with the legal aid society, I have been assigned to represent you in this case. Your mom is in the courtroom, I just wanted to come back here to let you know what would be happening." "Your docket number is fifth on the calendar list so you should be called quickly". The best I could do is throw ourselves at the mercy of the court, this confession is as tight as a monkey's ass and besides your legal guardian was there when you made it. You are going in front of an arraignment judge. we could ask that you be sentenced here and you might end up with a significantly lighter sentence. I ran it by your mother and she concurs". "Con what, I replied." "Concurs, It means she agrees with me". "Just sit tight, I am going to talk to the judge and the D.A. in chambers, I might be able to pull off a Harry whodini". He heads back through the courtroom door and I am left to sit there and wonder what is going to happen to me next. The only thing I could be sure of was that I was not going home tonight or any other night in the near future, he made that very clear. It seems I had fucked myself by running my mouth at the precinct. I don't know what they were talking about but they were taking a long time. The court officers were all huddled up in front of the court entrance door so I knew it was some kind of recess or something. An hour after that I would hear my name called. A big husky court officer with some fragile looking Hispanic officer came to the gate. "Shaheem Thomas on the gate, he yelled"." Stick your hand through the hole." I stuck my hands through the hole between the bars only for those hands to be returned to me with handcuffs on them. He opened the gate up and grabbed me by the left arm while the Hispanic officer grabbed me on the right. When I got to the edge of the courtroom door, I could see my mother and my aunt in the seats. This is one of the times in my life where I could say my mother showed she really cared for me. There were very few days after that were I could pinpoint her love. the officer knocked on the door with a heavy thump and said," case number 950.120 from the back, people vs. shaheem Thomas. I am led through the courtroom to the defendants chair next to my court appointed attorney. The judge has hair as white as snow. He looks like the person on bonanza but older. " what is the peoples recommendation in this case, the judge inquires?" the prosecutor responds, " your honor, it is the peoples position that this crime was not a crime of passion, or self defense, but rather your honor a crime of wanton disregard for human life. Considering the violent nature of the crime.. Were asking for a stiff prison sentence and extensive rehabilitation. The judge looks at him as if he is used to hearing this prosecutor over dramatize everything and says, "would that be all?' "yes, your honor', responded the prosecutor. The judge than turns to my lawyer and asks, defense, "do you have anything to say on your clients' behalf"? My lawyer responds enthusiastically, "Yes your honor I do". "I figured you would, you may proceed". "Thank you your honor. Before I go on your honor I'd like to direct the courts attention to the good book for a moment". The judge looks puzzled but nonetheless concedes, "Don't make this a sermon". "Yes your honor. We see that in the good book, a scenario between an adulterous woman and the religious leaders of the day. They sought to stone this woman for her wrongs and sought insight from Jesus concerning the matter. Jesus in his infinite wisdom knew this woman's wrongs were no different from the wrongs committed by every human being. So in the dust on the ground he wrote these words," let he who is without sin cast the first stone". "I guess what I am trying to say your honor is… yes. This young man wronged society but should he be put to death by way of a lengthy prison sentence? Should his life be cut short before it even begins? Your honor he is not even sixteen for Christ sakes. Keeping him in a cage will not right his wrongs; but a healthy environment, con-

ducive to learning and an opportunity will make him a pro-
ductive citizen in society. And with that your honor the
defense rests". The people in the seats were floored after that,
even my mother. They all felt like they were in a black church
on Sunday morning listening to their favorite sermon. The
prosecutor wasn't moved one bit. The judge gathered his
paper work up and said," with all that has been said here, and
the information contained in this jacket, I'm going to go to my
chambers and come back with a decision". He motions to exit
and the court officer gives us an order to rise. The judge exits
to his chambers. he sure didn't have much to read In there
because he came back out in less than five minutes. He
knocked on the courtroom door from his chambers to alert
the court officers that he was coming back in. "all rise. The
honorable judge David d. Rothway presiding. This court is
now back in session. The court comes to order and the judge
get right to business. "Counsel approach the bench". They
both go to the bench for a sidebar discussion. It was low so I
could vaguely make out what they were saying. I started to
read their lips and it became clearer. "I'm sure you're both
aware that although he is charged as an adult, he'll be sentenced under juvenile guidelines". My lawyer responds, "yes
your honor". The judge looks at the prosecutor," prosecution,
do you acknowledge this fact"? Prosecution gives his reluc-
tant acknowledgement," yes your honor we do, but we are
asking for the maximum sentence under those guidelines".
The judge orders them back to their respective stations in the
courtroom. "Alrighty, let s proceed, the judge orders, Mr.
Thomas, please rise". I stand up to take what was coming to
me. At the time, I was kinda numb. The judge looks at me
over the rim of his Benjamin Franklin glasses and asks, "Mr.
Thomas, do you have anything to say in your defense before I
give my decision?" I look at the judge, than around the room,
but words seem not to be able to come out. I drop my head
down, indicative that I had nothing to say. The judge looks
stunned and says, "Mr. Thomas, you have nothing to say? All

right. Mr. Shaheem Thomas, I find that your actions, reckless and haphazard. It shows you have no remorse or regard for human life. I hereby sentence you to seven and a half to fifteen years to be served under the youth division of corrections until your twenty-first birthday, at which time you will be sent to the state division of corrections. At this point, I became over-whelmed with fear. I drop back into my chair. I could hear my mother exploding with anger. "He's just a baby! Oh, god! Don't let them take my baby! Shaheem, shaheem! I don't move an inch. The world around me has gone silent. Everything around me is moving in slow motion. The two officers pull me up out of my seat and escort me to the exit back to the cell. Before they usher me back to the cell I get one last look at my mother. She frantically tries to get to me but is held back by court officers. The exit door slams shut.

I was immediately sent to Rickers Island to wait to be sent
upstate to a detention for youth. I was loused down with some
white substance, body cavity searched and given toiletries. I
was assigned a dorm and given a bunk number. When I
entered the dorm, everyone was at the gate waiting for me. It
seems like I was the new prize. My heart begins to pound out
of my chest. As I pass down the dorm by the other bunks, I
tried not to show fear. The sign of fear will certainly make my
time less comfortable, I would probably end up washing some-
ones'under wear. I knew that fear was like blood in the water
to sharks. I found my assigned bunk and sat down on it. I
stared across the room to make an assessment of what I was up
against. As I turn my head back to the front of the dorm, I am
startled by an inmate. "Yo, what's up baby boy, what they got
you down for?" "Looking at him intently I respond, Murder".
"Word... he retorts, you don't look like no murderer. You see
that nigga over there by the TV?" I motion toward the person he wants me to look at. "That's a murderer. Yo... He cut a
motherfucker guts out for bumping into his girl. I guess he
wanted me to be moved by his statement. I responded, "Its all
the same... a motherfuckers dead, and he aint coming back".
That didn't seem to stop him from running his mouth. He
continued on, "yeah, anyway, I just came to let you know, nig-
gas in here probably gonna try to move on you tonight for
those kicks. I know you don't have a lock, you aint been to
commissary. Yo, if you want, you can leave your shit in my
locker". This nigger has got to be crazy, where does he think
I'm from? "Good looking, but I can hold my own shit down.
I'm going all out for mine". "He senses I am not really the
classic candidate for the bullshit but continues anyway, "I'm

not saying you don't get down for your crown…. I'm irritated now, "aye, yo! I said I'm all right! He looks at me and begins to shake his head. He looks at the niggers standing by the bathroom and says, "I tried it the easy way…..fuck um. Do what ya'll gotta do". Just what I thought, that nigger didn't have my best interest at hand. He was down with the bullshit all along. I start to see niggers starting to huddle up more and more. I stand to my feet to prepare myself for whatever. They start filling the threshold of the bathroom door and covering the bubble. That is the place between the A & B gate where the officers sit and watch what goes on inside the dorm. Another inmate, different from the first one, approaches me and asks," what are you going to do for those kicks black?' "I look at him with an arrogance that he has never seen and say, "Whatever is clever baby Pa! He steps up into my space all in my face. Sweat begins to trickle down his face. Before he even realizes what hits him I give him a blow to his dome with the side of my fist so that I didn't hurt my knuckles. I than start punching him in the jaw. Out of nowhere like a pack of jackals. The other inmates begin to jump me, pounding me out like a pizza man pounds dough. I was being beaten severely. They pull off my sneakers while I lay there in the fetal position on the floor. To no avail, I tried to dodge their blows. One of the inmates appears with a razor slashing me several times across my back. I started screaming like a bitch that just loss her virginity. The scream echoes throughout the dorm. The inmates scatter in different directions, on different bunks. I somehow managed to get to my feet and stumble out to the gate. I collapsed in a pool of my own blood unconscious. When I awoke, I was lying on a table face down. There was a sudden sharp pain poking me every five seconds or so. I was being sewn up in the infirmary by the prison doctor. The local anesthesia is wearing off because I can feel the pain sharply. I look around and see several correction officers. I am also feeling kind of queasy and my head begins to droop back on the slab of iron. I tried to fight the pain of being poked with the needle by looking the other way. It is penetrating my flesh. Through the infirmary doors comes captain stokes. Captain stokes is a clean cut looking gentleman and hard ass at the same time. You can tell he is fucking all of the woman correctional staff. "Where is he, he asks,' talking about me?" "Is this Thomas, pointing to the other inmate who is suffering from a broken jaw?" The doctor looks at him and says, "No sir, right here, pointing to me". "Thomas, look, I'm not here for the rap session... I want some names and I want them now". I look at him as if he knows I know better and the response that he knows he is going to get. "I don't have any for you, and even if I did... I couldn't give them to you". "He is incensed by my defiance," if someone tenderized my back like that I'd want to get some justice out of it. The only way you are going to get that in my jail is Sinatra's way. My way!" Not cracking a smile I give him my same reply," I just told you, I don't have anything for you". "O.k. Billy bad ass, play it the hard way. He directs his attention to the other officer in the room and says, "When they finish patching his black ass up, I want him on ice until he melts". After I am patched up I am immediately taken to lock up, I guess this was punishment for taking an ass whipping and not telling on the perpetrators. I was on lock down for dam near a week before I was allowed to even have my clothes. I could hear screams from the other cells next to me from guys going crazy being in a cell all day twenty-four hours a day with the exception of a ten-minute shower. I would sit alone in my cell staring at the wall and roaches scurrying into the cracks in the wall. I hear a shrill squeaking of rusty wheels from the book cart rolling down the tier. I can hear him murmuring to other inmates inside their cells. "On the book call! I don't got no smokes, and I aint passing none either so don't ask". He reaches my cell at the end of the cellblock. The cart comes to a halt in front of my cell door. I look up to see him right outside of my door. "Aye, youngster, you want a book?" it gets lonely in that motherfucker all day, Everyday". This is the last one, you better take it". Up until that moment, I hadn't even realized that I was on the adult side of the building. This got dam captain upgraded my security level and they put me on the adult side of the building. I couldn't believe that shit. I didn't even know he could do that but come to find out he could. You see, I had a violent felon and my time was to be served as an adolescent and adult at the discretion of the institution. It basically meant if I got out of hand in the detention side of the joint than they could transfer me to the adult side. After my shock, I stood to reach between the bars and grab the book. "What is it, I ask, referring to the book I was receiving?" "He responded in a manner that indicated he was not in the mood for a whole lot of questions, "look, I'm the librarian. I bring em up and take em down; but for thirty-eight cents a day, I aint reading all those books down there. I think it's about some cracker from back in the day". The librarian leaves. I look at the title of the book, it's called, "the prince. By a dude named Machiavelli. I toss the book onto the bed. It slides off onto the floor between the bed and the wall. I slide the bed back and look under it to retrieve the book, which I would later call lost jewel. I picked it up and noticed a piece of paper on the floor. It is a torn out page of a porno magazine. I pick it up and check to see if anyone was around. I looked through the peep of the slit of my cell door. I took a dump and when I finished I took some toothpaste and posted the torn page on the wall. That was the first time I beat my meat in my life. It felt better than real sex because I didn't have to wait for anybody. I was staring into the mirror watching my facial expression as I was jerking off to give myself that extra boost. I guess you can say I was feeling myself. After I had finished I washed my hands and face in the dirty washbasin. The lights went out in my cell, it was obvious it was time to go to bed; at least the administration thought so. I could still see a little because my cell faced the yard so I put a piece of paper on one side of the cell window to harness the light so that it could be directly targeted on my bed. I start to read parts of the book aloud. The book seems to be taking me a place that I have never been

taken before. I am learning about what it takes to lead men
and how to watch out for snakes and suckers. This has been
the first time in my life that I have ever been inspired so much
by a book that I just want to become the person in the book. I
stayed up all night reading it and by morning I began to feel
like the prince that was described in the book. I must also say
that I became a veracious reader from than on out. I fell asleep
to the sun hitting me in the face like a bolt of lightening. That
night was like heaven for me. I had forgotten about all around
me. There were no walls or barriers. I was free in my mind and
my soul felt nourished. I knew I was changing, and I was
changing for the better,in some respects,and in others, I was
not. I was awakened by the kitchen inmate banging on my cell
door alerting me that chow was here. "Chow time, you eat-
ing?" I rise and go to the cell to retrieve my tray, all that reading made me hungry. The meal looked like vomit on a platter.
I tossed it on the concrete table and wash my face so I could
get the sleep out of my eyes. I hear a voice over the P.A. system; it is the voice of an officer. "Listen up, top tier cells, 1
through 25, odd numbers, shower time in 45 minutes. I look
at the food on the table, shake my head and begin to work out.
I knew that if I was going to get my mind right my body had
to be right right along with it. I was determined to come home
on some new and improved shit. I was on a mission to come
home demanding respect. I wanted people to see a change in
me the moment they saw me, both mentally and psychically. I
would spend many a years on solitary for many different rea-
sons, mostly fighting and sticking up for causes of the weak. I
was a seasoned criminal. The best time of my tour of duty in
the hellholes of the many prisons I was in was in my cell on
lock down. Although I had lost most of my good time, I was
not deprived because I was arming myself with a weapon that
could destroy bullets. I was being armed with a brain to think
rationally and cleverly. I went on to read great works like "the
art of war", by sun tsu and books on strategy, business, history and power. Ten years had passed and I didn't know where it

all went. I was going for parole today and the irony was that I was going from lock down. I was clean-shaven, bald by choice and an air of arrogance was all about me embodied in my personality. I had matured in the joint. My hands were rougher. I couldn't believe it was nineteen ninety-five. Time is at a stand still when you're incarcerated. I had no real sense of time. I mean I knew it was going forward, but I had no idea how things were progressing on the outside. Today was the day for me. I was either going to be a free man or I was coming right back to the cell to soak in disappointment. It didn't matter though; I was already turned down by parole before. My cell door opened and I am told to get dressed and go to A block for a hearing. I was already dressed. The parole board consisted of a five-panel board that all had to vote in favor of your parole or it would be denied. This board consisted of two woman and three men. I was waved inside by the black parole-hearing woman. I took a seat in front of the panel. The white lady officer shoots away first. "Mr. Thomas, you have been called down this morning to be heard on your suitability for parole at this time. The panel will ask you some questions, which you must answer. You may not answer until the question is asked completely. I also request that you carry yourself in the best conduct during this hearing. Is that understood?' I reply, yes maam, I understand. She fires away again," Mr. Thomas, why should you be paroled". I pause for a second to give my mind time enough to absorb the question and come back with an intelligent answer. "I should be paroled because I already have a life sentence knowing that innocent blood has been shed by my hands. I am totally reprehensible, from now until eternity. It will not make the pain of what I've done any less bearable. I know that my actions were morally wrong. I can only hope I am afforded the opportunity to make amends by deterring others from falling into this life, thereby saving several lives with one stone. That is why I should be paroled". I made sure I said everything they wanted to hear. I knew from my past experiences with them that you had to show remorse even if you didn't feel any. Play the game or the game will get played on you. I also knew I had to throw that religious transformation bit on them as well. There not buying your new-found disdain for crime if you don't mention that the man form up above had something to do with it. I am than hit with a question by one of the male panelist. "Alright. Mr. Thomas, I see your institutional record has more than your fair share of blemishes on it. In light of this fact what makes us think you're ready. I do see you have managed to secure a high school equivalency diploma and some college?" I ask myself how could I get around these tickets. I think for a second and than shoot from the hip and let my instincts be my guide. "Sir, for ten years I have been paying a debt to society that I myself don't think I can ever repay because a life was lost. I have come to understand that if life can be taken by my hands due to my ignorance, the least I can do is deter others from making the same bad decisions that I have made. My only solution was to better myself through the medium of education and to make choices that would better my situation and the situation of others. The panel is stunned; they had even forgotten the part about me having so many tickets. The art of persuasive speech is a motherfucker. The second woman on the panel gives her brief take, "uhm, we have no further questions. That will be all. You are excused". I am puzzled by the swiftness of the hearing. I believe I aced it but you can never tell. The rest of the panel was silent. Just as I exit the room, I could hear the stamp slam on my institutional folder. I would find out days later that it was a paroled stamp. I was on my way home after all those years.

4

It would be several weeks before my paperwork got back from Albany, giving me the go ahead to come home. They also had to insure I didn't have any outstanding warrants on me or anything. They could have the paperwork ready in days but instead they fuck with you by making you wait, and wait, and wait. I think it is just another tactic to keep you mindful of the fact that they own you and are very much in control of the situation. I was told by the eleven to seven shift that I was going home the next day, the only way they even knew was because they were ordered to have me off of the count for the morning. I wasn't going anywhere if I was still on the count. That is the one thing that is of the utmost importance in every prison and jail across America, that motherfucking count. If the count isn't right, no one goes anywhere until that motherfucker is right. They don't want to be responsible for no niggers running around town scaring white folk. I was in the cell all night pacing. I couldn't get any sleep. What was I going to see when I got out, was the world so evolved that I would not be able to catch up, how would I adjust to civilized society after I have been deprived of civility so long? The only thing I had going for myself was that I was a thinking man, an educated man in many respects. I had undergone what most inmates like myself consider the Malcolm X experience. I have crossed the burning sands of Arabia with Mohammed and spoke with Allah. I walked on the banks of the Galilee River with Jesus and fed five thousand lost souls. I found enlightenment with Buddha, and listen to philosophy from Confucius. I also talked and broke bread with a Tibetan Monk. I was ready for the world, the question was rather the world was ready for me or not? That morning at precisely seven forty-two A.M. the doors of my cell opened and closed behind me, simultaneously a new door opened, it was the door of opportunity; at least that is what I thought. I went downstairs to the processing area to get street clothes that I did not have because I didn't tell anybody I was coming home. I wanted it to be a surprise. I don't know how surprise they were going to be because I hadn't seen any of them in years. My mother would send letters and cards at first but eventually she became tired or should I say, life just kept on moving on the outside and she had no choice but to keep on moving right along with it. I wasn't mad at all though, nothing was going to fuck up my new beginnings, besides I had bought myself there. If I didn't learn anything else, I learned that I created my own set of unique circumstances. I was given thirty-three dollars by the property officer to get on the bus. Can you believe the clothes that I was arrested in were still in property? You would have thought they would have thrown that shit away. They'll treat you like shit your whole bit and care about you when your going home by saving your property. Shit, don't do me any favors. They didn't leave anything to chance either. They don't want you wandering around town up there in the boon docks. Black folk aint got no business upstate in those hick towns unless they are getting out of jail or going to visit somebody in one. They took me to the bus stop and made sure I was on board back to the city. It is amazing how much the little things mean so much to you when they are taken away from you. That bus ride made me feel like a faggot in boys land. Shit I had just got out of jail, that was the last thing I needed to be feeling like. I didn't blink all the way back to the city. I watched the soft wind blow through the cornfields and the new cars that were on the highway. The people on the bus knew I had just come out of prison, for one I looked like everything was new to me, and it was, secondly I still had on prison greens. I saw a dead deer on the highway, which was the first time I had seen a deer up close. I guess it tried to cross from one side to the other and got run over. When I arrived at the port authority, I knew shit was popping in the city. I had just read the autobiography of Malcolm X several months back so I knew how he felt when he boarded a train to New York and saw all of the hustle and bustle of the big city. I felt like a kid again for a minute up until the time I walked out of the bus station and saw those big brown cap letters engraved on the front of the building across the street that read," new York state division of parole". This shit had to be by design. They want you to be mindful the moment you set foot back in New York that you are being watched. I started looking behind me to see if there were any big stocky looking men with bulging side pockets indicative of their guns in holster or a puffy T-shirt because their bullet proof vest was too big for them. You had twenty-four hours to contact parole once you got out. I figured I might as well get this shit over with since I was down here already rather than have to come right back down here in the morning. It was jam packed in there, a sea and ocean of niggers. There are only four places that niggers rein supreme, that's prison, parole, the grave, and hell. I went to the front desk to make my presence to the staff known. The security guard instructed me to sign in ,take a seat and wait for a parole officer to call me. I was in there for hours when finally a big white man who looked like he ate a box of dunkin donuts a day called my name," shaheem Thomas", I look and respond in kind," right here". "Get your stuff and follow me to my office". I grabbed my bag, which was nothing more than things I had made in jail and books, a few letters as well. I sat down in the chair that was obviously designated for parolees. He cut right to the meat and bones of it all and said," look, you're a parolee and I am a parole officer. You have a job to do and that job is to stay out of trouble. I have a job to do and that job is to make sure that if you fuck up I am there to scoop you up and throw your blackass back in jail. I'm not here to be your father, lover of friend". I am saying to myself this is going to be like being in jail all over again. I hadn't been in the city more than five hours and I was back in jail, at least mentally.

He further instructed me to be down there every Monday and to stay clear of drugs because he would be giving me random piss tests. I was to look for suitable employment and steer clear of criminal activities and the criminal element. Was this motherfucker crazy, how the fuck am I going to steer clear of the criminal element when I live smack dab in the heart of crime. I took the paper he had given me outlining the conditions of my parole and I bounced to the train station to get uptown. I jumped on the two train to 135th street and Lenox ave, in front of Harlem hospital. The hospital looked the same to me, shit it looked this way every since they shot the shaft scene here. With the addition of a few new stores, there was nothing that really changed. I guess it's true, the more things change, the more they remain the same. I don't know what those old time niggers coming home from around my way were seeing, I can't see a bit of a difference out here. I walked down 135th street towards Madison Avenue. I made sure not tot cut through the projects because I didn't want anybody to see me in greens. When I got to the corner of 135th street and Madison Avenue, I could see my old window. It had a make shift curtain in the form of a sheet stuck in between a crack in the window. As I made my way to the elevator I knew I was definitely back home again. The elevator smelled like pure D piss. When I got to my floor, I hesitated to knock on the door in fear of what type of response I would get from the other side. I finally get up the courage to knock on the door. The door flies open and the screams of surprise! Could be heard all the way to the first floor. How the hell did they know I was coming home today? I step in the door and I see welcome home plastered all over the place. My sister Debra hugs me as if she is squeezing the life out of a teddy bear as I look on in disbelief at what is going on and how big she has gotten. I was shocked and embarrassed at the same time. "How did you guys know I was coming home, I asked"? Debra responds with the obvious," somebody from the parole division made a home visit to make sure you would be living here... who cares how we found out anyway, your home and that's the best part". I hug her again and smile but it doesn't hide my apparent uneasiness. 'where's ma", I ask, in a concern manner, assuming she would be here to greet her baby boy; after all it has been only ten years. No one says a word but hint in the direction of her bedroom. I walk slowly to her room as if I was walking the last mile on my way to a death row gas chamber. As I edge towards her bedroom, I could see my mother looking in the mirror. I could see my reflection in her mirror. A sudden smile comes across my face; it is the smile of a baby boy running to his mothers arm after a fall in the park. My mother turns as I inch toward her and embraces me. "Mama". "my son is home. A truly blessed day the lord has made. Now my soul can truly rest". I give her reassuring words," I'm home ma... and I am going to take care of you, I promise. "Shaheem ...baby, I don't want you hanging around with those same fools from around here. They liable to get you in trouble again". I don't know if she was referring to those fools polo and Tracey or a new set of fools but she certainly had my ear. I responded and was cut off In my tracks, Ma, look, I'm not... she puts her hand on my lip to hush," shaheem, there is nothing more important in this world than your freedom and your self-respect. You hear me"? I affirmed what she said, "Yes ma am , I know. "Good. I'm so glad to see you. You look beat. Go and get some sleep. I'll send everybody home. They can talk to you later". "Okay", I replied. Ma, thanks for everything, I promise you ma... I'm never going back". My mother smiles and exits out of the room. I go to my room down the hall. Amazingly it is relatively just like I left it, strange but that's the truth. I drop my bag and the floor and sit on the edge of the bed just to take it all in. looking around the room trying to bring back old memories. I go to the window to look outside to see the beautiful lights of Yankee stadium. I loved that the most about my room, the lights that lit up Yankee stadium. Over in the closet is a suit with my name on it, I guess my mother didn't want to leave anything to chance. I guess that is also a cue to get my ass up in the morning to go and look for a job. I don't see any problem with that, I am ready for the world and tomorrow I am going to go out there and get myself something. For right now, I am going to pull off my clothes and go to sleep. I close my door and call it a rap for the night. I am going to need a lot of rest to hit the pavement tomorrow in full force.

5

When I woke up the next morning, I was ready for the world. It was the dawn of a new day for me and also new beginnings. The sun had hit my face as if it was speaking to me to go out there and get my piece of what god had wanted me to have. That night was the first night in many years I had had a good nights sleep. I adjusted to home life just that fast. I was comfortable and my guards were obviously down. The clock radio read six thirty nine a.m. I went in the bathroom, brushed my teeth and took a long shower. I stood in front of the bathroom mirror for like an half an hour just looking at myself. The house was as quiet as a church mouse. I went back in my room, put on the clothes that was on the hanger for me and prepared for what lie ahead. When I went in the kitchen, there was some hi ho crackers wrapped in tin foil and coffee on the table. There was also a note with money on it indicating that it was mine to travel back and forth to look for a job and have lunch. My sister had created copies of a resume for me. It basically had the information that they already had since I sent home my equivalency diploma and college degree home. She made it look like I had worked at her job for a spell. I was rather prepared going out to look for work, probably more than the average; not to mention it was my first day on the set. Most niggers I know will lay up for months before they would even think of looking for work, I was up and out in a day flat. I decided I would get the daily news and hit a few job agencies. Every agency I went to made me fill out a long questionnaire. I wouldn't even make it past the next phase because the moment they saw the box checked off about me having a felony conviction the moment they would come up with an excuse as to why I would not be a right fit, I thought

their were laws against shit like that. I walked all the way
downtown by city hall; I mostly walked because I wanted to
just see the world around me. I saw a sign in front of the building directly in back of city hall that read" New York city housing authority is looking for you". I decided to go in and have
a look-see, maybe they were looking for me. I went upstairs to
the housing administrations floor; it was packed with niggers
waiting to be seen for an interview. I was the only nigger there
with a suit on, shit I was the only nigger there with a resume
in hand. I knew I was on my way. I went up to the front desk
and was immediately asked by the receptionist," are you here
for the employment fair for housing?" " yes, maam, I am ', I
replied. " than I am going to need you to fill out this application and questionnaire form and when your name is called follow the green line to the door that says interview". I filled out
the questionnaire and application and returned it to her. I was
called about a half an hour later. I followed the green line and
saw the sign in front of a ladies office by the name of Mrs.
Delaney. She is a beautiful black woman with luscious big lips
that you would just want to kiss all over. "Mr. Thomas, I have
briefly looked over your application and I see you have an
associate's degree in liberal arts and bachelors in business
administration. Are you sure you're applying for the right job?
I mean, there are other positions in our organization that can
accommodate and utilize your skills". I am thinking to myself,
I know this but I want to shoot low so that they would have no
reason to tell me no. "The maintenance position is perfect for
me right now, Mrs. Delaney. As you can see, I am more than
qualified to sweep floors and mop hallways. She looked aston-
ished at my reply and responded in the affirmative," I can't
argue with that... well, I guess that settles it. When can you
start"? Shit, start, I guess she is telling me I got the job, you
don't ask a nigger when can he start if you have no intention
of hiring him. "As soon as possible",I replied. "So, okay, be at
this address on Monday morning, 9:00 a.m. sharp. I was excit-
ed as hell; I had landed a job in one day.' Thank you ma am .

Thank you very much. The interview is apparently over from there. I rise to leave the office, ecstatic as can be at my good fortune. Just as I reach the door, the unthinkable comes. "Oh, Mr. Thomas, I'll just need you to sign here and check box number 16. Shit, I knew it was too dam good to be true, we all know what box number sixteen was. I hesitantly took the application and checked off the "yes" and hand her back the application for her final approval and inspection. She looks it over and her expression changes from one of excitement to disappointment. "Mr. Thomas, I'm very sorry, but the city's' policies state that any individual hired for a city agency position must have a clean record. I was just floored, I pleaded, "Mrs. Delaney, what am I supposed to do? If the city doesn't want to hire me, what can I expect from the private sector? If I can't even sweep your floors, who's' floor can I sweep? Tell me that Mrs. Delaney! "Her response was much the same as before," Mr. Thomas... I'm sorry, but those are the rules and policies set. I'm so sorry. "Yeah, me too", I responded in disgust. I turned my back on her and headed out of the office. I decided that my search for a job would end with this one today. I jumped on the express four train on the Lexington avenue line and headed for home. People were entering and exiting the train and I was completely oblivious to their every move, I was in my own little world trying to make sense out of what just happened; shit I knew what happened, society hadn't forgiven me. The train finally pulls up at 125th street and Lexington Avenue by the AK housing projects. My face looked like I had just lost my best friend. I head around the corner towards Park Avenue to see if the coffee shop was still there where the dope fiends hang out and take methadone. I could faintly hear a voice but I wasn't sure whether I was imagining it or it was real. I look up and there is a male figure around my age calling my name and looking me in the face at the same time. His voice sounds familiar but I just couldn't make it out. "Sha, sha! Its you, oh shit! My mother fuckin man. When you come home nigger?"I am immediately taken back to my child hood days. It is coming back to me. Emotions of hate, disgust and joy engulf my body all at the same time. Its, Tracey. He extends his hand to mine for a pound. I look at him as if I was a scanner at an airport, looking him up and down. "I came home last night. Why do you care? I aint hear shit from you niggers when I was up north". "Yo black, he responded, we was young. Shit was fucked up the way it went down, yo, but what you expected us to do"? This motherfucker doesn't even know what he did wrong so I had to explain it to his dumb ass, "you could have sent me a kite or two jackass. You could have shown a brother some love". I paused for a second and let loose a smile, after all it was ten years ago, this nigger didn't know any better. I put him at ease," it's all good my nigger, I know you didn't know better. I can only hope that you a tenth more of the man than you was ten years ago". I give him my hand and embraced him. We both move to the awning under the bodega. We continue in our pleasantries so to speak. "My mother fucker! So what you doing? Aye yo, sha, me and p-lo got shit locked in the projects kid". I'm thinking to myself, what's this p-lo shit. Niggers is grown men with silly ass nicknames. Tracey pulls out a knot of cash big enough to choke a horse. He peels off several bills and hands them to me. I look at him for a moment after examining the money, I hadn't seen big faces before, when I went away ten dollars was the most I ever had. I take the money happily as if that had erased all the pain both of those niggers had caused me ten years earlier. "Put that in your pocket. You came home at a good time my nigger. Me and P-lo put something together that's going to set a nigger up proper for life. We got a crew that aint having it kid! Yo, I got a position for you. Come to the spot tonight so I can introduce you to everyone. Plus, you know polo want to see a mother fucker'. I write the address down on a piece of paper and hug him good-bye. He gives me his parting salutation, "peace out yo. Sha, it's good to see you my nigger". I look at the address again to make sure I knew where it was while he walked towards First Avenue probably on his way to Wagner projects. I turned the corner on 125th street and Park Avenue to head uptown eight blocks to my house. When I got to my crib, I just took off my clothes and laid down.

6

When I woke up it was time to meet my new destiny. I had thought about it on my way uptown after I had left Tracey. I even thought about it in my dreams during my brief nap. I rationalized, why should I be so concerned with trying to do the right thing if society didn't want to give me a chance. I tried as far as I was concerned. I put back on my greens and a white T-shirt and left for the address where Tracey and polo were. The paper that I had written the address on read, 950 west 120th street. It was in walking distance so I headed to 120th street going down fifth avenue cutting through Mount Morris Park. The building was on morning Side Avenue. It was a descent looking brownstone building. I knocked on the door and someone came to the peephole and looked at me with this piercing look that indicated he was checking me out for something. Behind the door someone answers my request for admission via my knock on the door," who"? "Its shaheem, I replied, is Tracey there"? There is a slight pause. The peephole slides shut and several locks are being unlocked. The door flies open and polo stands there. For a split second, my mind flashes back to the scene in the grocery store when we were kids. Staring at polo's' face intently I jolt back to reality. Polo yells at me, "sha!" "Yeah, it's me in the flesh". "he takes a step back," I never thought it would take this long to see you nigger". He pulls me inside and locks the reinforced doors behind us. "You was right here all the time though, pointing to his heart, pounding on it with his right fist". "I had to let him know how I felt, just like I let Tracey know when I saw him. "If I was right here, pounding my heart, how come you never sent me no kite"? He pauses for a second as if rehearsing the statement to come and says," I aint going to front, when a nigger is locked down, its hard to write. I mean you just keep sayin the same ole shit. I figured if I was in a position to help you when you came home, you know, that would cover a multitude of sorrow. You following me"? I look at him showing him a slight contempt because I knew it was bullshit, but I had to give him a pass for the bullshit as I was given a pass for my bullshit ten years ago by the detectives on the case. "Yeah I follow you, I responded" we both kinda left it at that. We walk into the living room section of the house. It's dark and Smokey with several guys sitting in an arrangement that resembles a round table set up. Many of the men in the click are doing many different things at the table. Some are smoking while others are counting what appear to be mounds of cash. Some are also dispensing vials of crack into plastic bags. It is apparent polo and Tracey are in full control of this operation. Polo introduces me to the people at the table. "Listen up niggers. I want to introduce y'all to a long time homey of mines. He is bone of my bone and flesh of my flesh..." I look at him from the corner of my eye. Tracey steps on the other side of me while polo continues to give what appears to be a speech. "He's a G from the heart and we can all learn a lot from him. Sha, this is the click". "I give them a short "what's up". There is a kid loading bullets with his bare hands, his name was Murder rob. I had to let him know there was a brighter way to his madness. "My man, try doing that with gloves, it works". Polo throws his arms around my shoulders," yo, see what I told y'all mother fuckers! He knows his shit". "Tracey interjects, sha, you gotta make this move with us". I felt like he was planning this whole shit all along. I had to let both of them know this was not ten years ago and I learned my lesson from making moves with them. "Wait a minute. You and polo keep talking about making moves, but nobody is giving me any details". Tracey and polo look at each other for a spell than Tracey responds to my inquiry," y'all lounge for a while. We got to brief our man here". We walk to another room that is way in the back of the brownstone. I take a seat in the first chair next to the door; I guess it was prison

instincts. Tracey explains," aight, here's the deal. Those bodi-
quas on Broadway are only dealing with a pocket full of black
motherfuckers and that group of so-called "choice niggers"
are trying to dominate the set by holding out on the product.
We want to put pressure on them tight enough to get in with
these banana-eatin motherfuckers. My mind immediately
generates questions, after all, I had read the prince and the art
of war in prison, I was supposed to ask questions, especially
knowing the type of niggers I was dealing with. "And how do
you propose to do that without bringing heat on yourselves?
In addition to that, with all of those niggers you got in there,
how you going to keep one of them from dropping a dime on
your ass if the heat gets unbearable?" I can see they didn't
think this thing through like they should have. They never do,
I wouldn't have gotten ten years if they used their seven
ounces. Polo asserts his opinion," that's all the more reason
why we need you with us on this. Yo, one way or the other this
is going to happen". I am looking at him like, nigger what
were you going to do before you knew I was home. I look him
over as he continues to sell me on the idea. "I'd rather it happen with you and all. You had time to think about shit like this,
right?" I start to stare at him because of that comment. Tracey
smacks him in the mouth lightly to let him know he was talking too much. "So are you in, Tracey asks?" I stand and walk
over to the window to look out of it. I started to think about
my failed job search earlier in the day and all of the rejections
despite my efforts. "Yeah, I'm in," fuck it, at this point there
isn't much I could do. Employers already let me know where
I stood with them. My job search today let me know where I
stood in terms of society. It was now time I made a stand for
myself and afford myself an opportunity the only way I was
going to realistically get one. I agreed but I made sure to agree
only on the conditions that I set. We head back into the room
where I made it very clear that shit would have to go down the
way I wanted it to go down. I made my demand clear," everything has to be done exactly as I map it out. No deviation from

the plan, not one iota. First, I'm going to need all the information possible on these cats. I need hang out locations, place of residences, everything. "They responded in kind, "it's all good' polo confirms, "You got it". Tracey also concurs," aight yo, so go home and wait for me. I'll bring you everything you need to get things moving. Yo, sha, thanks black". I look at him for a minute and respond, "yeah, right". I give a head nod indicating I was down with it and head toward the door. I hug both Tracey and polo and make my way back uptown to my crib where I go straight to my bed and kick off my shoes.

7

Lying on my bed, staring at the ceiling I start to reflect back and fourth about a myriad of things, namely prison, to the disaster of an interview earlier, to meeting up with Tracey and polo's people. What really penetrates my brain is that fateful day ten years prior. I feel so empty and confused. My sister knocks on the door," sha, polo's at the door. You better tell him to stop banging on the door like that. Your lucky ma aint home. If ma knew about his ass coming over here..." deb, I'll take care of it okay. She rolls her eye, "you better". I walked to the door to open it. Polo is standing in front of my door with all grins. I step into the hallway and pull the door behind so that Debra is not in my business. "Polo you need to have some respect for a mans place. This aint Bosnia and shit". "Sorry, black. This is everything you asked for and than some. Yo, I even got their shit schedules. Sha, I got to take care of something so here you go, black handle your business. I'll check you tomorrow, same bat place, same bat time. Polo leaves and I re-enter my apartment and lock the door behind me. I head directly to my room. Debra is sitting on her bed studying. I look at her for a moment and head back to my room. I close the door, lay the paperwork on my bed and spread it out so I could get an overall view of what I had in my possession. The page has four names on them: fat jack, Chad, Ronnie, and Lynn. I glance through the pages, get out a pen and start taking notes and the information that I had before me. I am looking at the material as if mahacvelli would look at it. I am applying the principles I had learned from reading books on the art of war and strategy. I notice distinct charac- teristics in all of them. I notice from what I have here, fat jack never leaves his game room. He must be guarding something big in there. He sells weight from there, which means hitting it at the right time will yield cash and drugs in abundance. Chad is a flamboyant old timer who can be seen on any given day strolling up and down 125th street looking for attention and affirmation of who he is. That makes my job easier to get his ass. Ronnie is a young hustler who loves motorcycles and cars. He can be found in one or the other. Lynn is the tricky one, although he never leaves his house, it makes him easier to be found, but a man in his own environment is dangerous. I beep polo after going over all of the information after I came up with a workable plan. I tell him to tell him and his boys to meet me at their spot in the morning.

I woke up early that morning as I had awaken early the day before, this time is was not to look for a job but to do a job. I hadn't spent anytime with my mother because I was out all day last night. I felt like I was making a move that was going to allow me to have time to spend time with her and pay her back for just being my mother. I left my crib walking down the same route I had taken yesterday, down Fifth Avenue through Mount Morris Park. On the way there I am encountered by none other than detective hartsfield. He pulled up along side of me in a maroon classic Capri. I instantly knew it was him. He has one of those faces that you just don't forget. In a superficial inquisitive tone he asks," Mr. Brown?... oh, yeah,that's you. Harlem's' number one thug is on the streets. You look a little older but I know you're the same little, no good juvenile delinquent from a time not long ago". I am patiently listening to everything he has to say but letting it go in one ear and out the other. I sarcastically reply, "Are you finished detective?" He rebuts with his own brand of sarcasm," No, are you finished. That is the question. I'm gonna say this one time. Mr. Thomas... don't come out thinking you gonna fuck up my streets anymore than what they are cause I'll be watching you, you hear me?" I keep my eyes fixated on him, but not responding. I start to walk away and detective hartsfield yells another sarcastic insult, "shaheem, keep your eyes on the prize". I suck my teeth and keep it moving to my destination. I had no time to hear what he was saying; after all, he was coming at me sideways. I reach the spot and everyone is there waiting for me. I have the set of altered blueprints that I had received from polo that will outline the operation. I lay it across the roundtable and begin to explain it. "What you have here before you is the exact way this operation is to go down, but it is on paper. In order for it to work successfully you'll have to execute it to the letter. Now based on these guys character traits I have designed a formula to get the maximum out of the situation. I focused on their weaknesses rather than their strengths". As I am describing the events as they will unfold I can see all of the players involved gesturing as if they are all forming mental images of the way in which it will be carried out. I continue," this guy fat jack, he never leaves the game room, which means the stash is there also. Three of you will be responsible for getting the work and locking him in that game room. Take out all of the phones and gag him; leave the rest to me. This guy Chad is out in the public eye like gotti or something. He feels protected around the people. He'll have to be taken in the open. There is no two ways about it. I prefer when he gets his morning coffee and hash browns from mc Donald's. Why? Less people are there bring him directly here and don't answer any questions he may have, or even speak, for that matter. The rest, I'll deal with. And whatever you do, don't take anything other than the work from jack. Polo, Tracey, come with me". We all leave the spot to handle our business and our respective tasks that I had just given. Tracey and polo are unaware of it at this time but my anger against them has not been quenched yet for what they done to me ten years prior. I am setting a trap for them and they don't even know it. There is only going to be one winner in this whole ordeal. My only concern at this point was to make them look like accomplices in all of the murders that were about to be committed. I had planned all night that I was going to trade in the dope for money and use that to take care of my family. I never really forgot how they abandoned me and persuaded me to stick up that grocery store all by my lonesome. To me, crime was my only life now and it was because of the both of them that my life had taken such a dramatic turn. I had told frank nitty, one of their boys, to put on a meter man uniform I had seen in the back room. It was the perfect way to get inside fat jacks game room. He had agreed and it worked like a charm. He went right in there and knocked on the window that separated customers from himself and flashed an I.D, "uncle ed sent me down to check the meter", he said to jack. Jack was somewhat hesitant. He examined frank nitty looking him up and down until he was satisfied that he was in fact a meter man. He summons his worker to open the door. His worker is told by a flash of fat jacks hand to conceal the weapon he had in plain view. Once the door is opened it is apparant to both of them that it was the wrong decision to let him in. jack is wondering why the meter man has not gone to the back to check the meter. Just as he expects foul play, frank nitty pulls out his forty-five caliber with a silencer on it and shoots the doorman in the stomach. He goes down. Jack is now shitting bricks and begging for his life as frank lets his cronies in. frank hits him with the butt of the gun and stakes his claim," ah-ight mother fucker, you know what this is. Don't' start no shit and there won't be none". Fat jack is still begging, "God don't kill me, please don't kill me!" nitty is not moved by the tears, "shut the fuck up. You wasn't crying selling that ounce you just sold a minute ago". In a humble submissive tone jack pleads, "Look, take the money; it's under the freezer, right there. Take it! It don't mean nuthin to me. I got a daughter I want to see grow up". Frank tries to add a little humor, "then if you would be so kind as to tell me where the work is I think you gonna live to see your precious one graduate". In a phony sense of shock as if he doesn't know what he was talking about jack says," what work"? He fucked up when he did that. Frank was more incensed, "now that's the wrong answer! Try again. Fat jack is now bleeding from the mouth," man I'm telling you, the work is finished. I sold the last of it". Just as he completes his sentence, franks' crony finds the work. Booda is holding the two bags full of dope," bingo! I found the jack pot, no pun intended". Frank is boiling," you lied to me fat ass. You don't have any respect for me. What have I done to deserve this? I thought you were my friend". He looks at his boys and instructs them on what to do next," tie his ass up and take him to the back. Make sure he's tied tight". Meanwhile he is ripping the phones out of the socket. He calls for the other two and they lock the joint up leaving fat jack inside. They all jump in the car back to the spot to drop off the two kilos of dope before picking or snatching up Chad. They are all in the car discussing the situation. Frank is happy as hell," I don't' know about ya'll but these two bricks of dope we got is a lot to smile about. We got over a million dollars in our possession". Murder rob adds his two cents," fuck that right now. I'm thinking about the stupid shit we just did'. Booda is looking at him as if he is crazy," did you hear what that man just said? We got over a million dollars in our possession. Don't nothing sound fucked up about that. Frank now turns to rob," yeah nigger you trippin right now, open the window and catch your breath". He hits right back, trying to get them to understand the gist of what he was trying to say," trippin? I'm trippin? Man, we just left a motherfucker alive that had over a million dollars worth of work. Fuck that, turn around". Frank, looking at him in utter shock," nigger, you stone cold crazy! Rob insists," turn around, yo. We going to do this my way. I aint leaving no boogie man around to haunt me later". Booda looks at him," our instructions were to tie him up and leave him alive". "Fuck those instructions. Turn the fuck around!" They reluctantly turn around and head back for the candy store. Murder rob gets out," give me the keys and stay right here. I'll be right out". Frank hands him the keys. Murder rob takes them, goes inside and shoots fat jack twice in the head. He notices that fat jack still has his Rolex on. He takes it off of his wrist and puts it in his pocket. He comes back out and gets in the car. They drive off. "Now was that hard, he asks?" franks responds," yeah you damn right. Now we got a body that could have been taken care of by someone else. Rob is not concerned with his sentiments, "yeah whatever. We got bodies anyway. One more aint gonna hurt". Uptown in park Chester polo, Tracey, and me are at Ronnie's house. It is away from the hood in a quiet suburban environment. Ronnie is in the house with a bitch getting his dick sucked. You can see right through his window. He has on a robe and she is as naked as the day she was born. The three of us are in the car waiting for the proper moment to run up in there on his ass. Polo has binoculars and is looking dead in his crib, "dam that bitch can swallow a dick!' Tracey snatches the binoculars from polo, "let me see... now that's a fine asshole. Ugly niggers get all the good pussy when they got money". I ask for the binoculars so I could see for business purposes, "let me see for a second. It's on. Now is a better time than ever to roll up in there. I hope we catch him busting a nut". We all get out of the car and approach the house from the back. Instead of breaking any doors or anything, we use electronic scramblers to pen the garage door and enter the house. Tracey trips over an electronic cord making a little noise. I whisper, "shhhh!... you want him to know were here?" we go upstairs, making our way to the living room where Ronnie and the freak are. He is fucking her in the ass. I hear her saying," ooh! Ooh!...fuck me daddy, cum inside me daddy. "Ronnie's ego is out of this world, "cum is what you want, cum is what you gonna get". Simultaneously while he is Cumming and she is Cumming, we all walk into the living room. I am pointing the gun at Ronnie and simulating the voice of a male and female climax, "ooh, ah, woo-wee! I hope it felt good for you as it did for me'. Ronnie reaches for his gun that is on the nightstand by him. Was he crazy, "now don't you go making a bad situation worse, I said, get your mother fuckin hands up. You too bitch. Polo get his gun. He is not going to need it". Polo recovers Ronnie's gun from the nightstand. "Tracey put these on his ass, as I hand him the hand cuffs to cuff him with". Ronnie is trying to figure this all out," I don't know what the fuck this is all about but if you disappear in five minutes I'll forget this little incident ever occurred. We all start to laugh at that shit. Tracey had to add his stand up act to the equation,' you can forget from now until Armageddon. Reality will help jog your memory cause we aint going nowhere". Ronnie is trying to reason with us at this point, "what the fuck do you want money? I'll give you money, say ten thousand a piece? Polo makes it plain for him," we don't want money. We want a cut from your spots uptown, and we want to be plugged in with your second family on Broadway". Ronnie knows that is not an option," now you know I can't do that. That's like signing my own death certificate". I had other means of making him agree to our demands," oh you will do it, and I'm going to give you just the right dosage of incentive to do it". I point the gun back at his face. 'Bend him over that table right there", I instructed. "Sha, what are you going to do", polo asked. "Just bend him the fuck over, I aint got time for games". I look into my bag and pull out a Polaroid camera. I walk over to Ronnie and begin to pull down his pants. Tracey gets the picture of what is about to happen," yo, I know you just came home and everything but you don't have to go out like that". ' shut the fuck up", I ordered". Ronnie is begging softly," don't do it man. My manhood is all I got". "That's why I'm taking it," I said, now if you cooperate I'll destroy these pictures. If you don't, I'll plaster these up in every hood within a ten mile radius of Harlem". Ronnie begins to scream because of the pain of penetration. Polo sarcastically remarks, "I guess it's safe to ask where the money is now!" 'It's in my room, in a safe behind my bed". "Well lets get to stepping", I insisted. We exit the living room and head for the bedroom. "What's the combo?" I asked? Ronnie reluctantly replies, "twenty-eight right, thirty six left, all the way around twice than four right". 'Bingo', I shouted. My eyes almost popped out of my head looking at all that cash, "now see, this is incentive enough for me to keep hush, hush about these pictures". "You got what you want; take it, its yours". "Oh we plan to", Tracey asserts. I looked at polo and told him to bag that shit up so we could get the fuck outta there. "Are you going to kill me", Ronnie asked. I put his mind at ease," fuck no, I need you alive. You think I just finished digging your guts out for nothing. I'm gonna pimp you like a hoe on Broadway, or else". 'Or else what, Ronnie asks? 'Or else those pictures go out, that's what. Meanwhile, don't call us, we'll call you". We exit the bedroom and I instruct Tracey and polo to cut the phone lines. Ronnie has the look of a woman who has just been beaten and humiliated by her man. He's too ashamed to utter a word to anyone. We go to the car and make our way back to the spot.

9

unbeknownst to me ,on the other side of town rob and booda had not only fucked things up ,but apparently somebody left the candy store gate up when I gave specific orders to pull it down. I also found out it was rob. Apparently he left it open after he went back to kill him, another wrong move. Little kids thought the store was open and went in and found jack and his man dead as a door nail. The kid was banging on the glass, "fats, hurry up. I need four quarters". He notices the door inside the store is slightly ajar, "fats, you in there"? He looks around sensing something is wrong. He goes in and finds both bodies sprawled across the floor with fats head oozing white mass. No sooner than finding the bodies police are on the scene. The regular police get there first than super cop gets there with his partner. "What do ya got?" detective harts field asks the detective on the scene. "You got a one Michael Barnes, a.k.a. fat jack, laid out with a bullet in his head in the back of his own establishment, that's what you got. Hartsfield wants to solve this in a hurry, "any leads"? Sarcastically he replies, "A lead to nowhere. We got a clean bullet casing, probably wiped off before they got here, a store full of fingerprints. Problem is, this is a game room and a candy store. People buy candy and people play games. And a couple of kids who say they haven't seen shit. I think that narrows it down to about a billion suspects in the naked city". That seems like an unacceptable answer to hartsfield. That wasn't the one he was looking for. "Where are the kids now"? he asks. The detective points to a group of kids standing on the side walk and says, "Over there". Hartsfield puts on his best Sherlock Holmes face and walks over to the kids. "Alright, which one of you's want to make a crisp ten dollar bill"? The first kid that

answered was obviously the baddest ass out of the group," it
all depends. What we gotta do for it? No snitches over here,
if that's what you mean". He didn't know it but that was the
response hartsfield needed to reel him in. "then you must
know something. You can't snitch if you don't know nothing".
The second kid lends his smart retort, "well technically, we
don't know nothing". "Well not so technically, what do you
know", asks hartsfield? The first kid signals to the second kid,
"Shut up, you talk too much". Hartsfield is now getting vexed,
"I don't have time for games. I'll take all your little asses
downtown and make your mammas get out of beds to come
get you. Now take this ten and gimme what I need". That was
enough for one of the kids to start talking. "When we got here
earlier a guy was in front of the store giving us money to come
back later". Hartsfield knows he is getting somewhere now.
"Do you remember what he looked like"? The young man
holds his hand to his head as if trying to recall the mans face
and than says, "he was dark skinned with a mole next to his
eye'. "Is that it"? "Yeah, that's it. You got twenty dollars worth
of information for ten dollars". "Than sue me than", he replies
to the little derelict. Hartsfield begins to walk off and as he
takes a couple of steps, the kids grab on his jacket. "Detective',
one of them shouts. "Yeah kid". He offers some more information in hopes of retrieving his bounty, "one other thing, I
noticed that fats didn't have his watch on when I found the
body", they must've took it". harts field begins to salivate,
"what, was it a special kind of watch"? "Hell yeah, he
responds, it was a Rolex flooded with diamonds". Hartsfield
is satisfied with what he gets from them by way of information. He goes in his pocket and pulls out a twenty-dollar bill
and hands it to one of the kids, "you see, it pays to snitch
sometimes". He gets into his car with his partner and drives
off. Meanwhile, shaheem, polo and all of the other members
of their crew are back at the spot. The three members that
went to take care of fat jack are already at the table. Money
and dope is on the table. Polo, Tracey, and me come in with

our bags of money and dump it on the table. Everybody sits but me. Because I orchestrated everything most at the table see me as the leader and hero, like I knew they would. I am ready to make a profound speech as I glance across the table at the spoils, "behold, this is your key to liberation. This is your way out. As long as you keep it real with each other, you will always have it. In America, it's a fight for peace, freedom and money. We have made war so that we may have peace. Enjoy my niggers, enjoy". They all go crazy at the table. I feel like Hitler giving a speech to his nazi regime. They all start playing with the money, lighting cigars, popping moet and even sniffing some of the dope. I pull nitty to the side to discuss how everything went at fat jacks candy store. I call him over to me, "main man, let me talk to you a minute". We both go into the back room. He is looking suspicious as to why I singled him out. "What's up, he asks"? I get straight to the point, "everything went down alright, did you make sure you clipped the wires"? "It went somewhat kosher". I am puzzled, I know what that means. "What do you mean somewhat kosher"? ""rob killed him", he blurted. "He did what, trying not to take in what he just said"? "I wasn't about to argue with a nut with a loaded gun. He goes postal when he don't get what he wants. Anyway, we should've never taken rob anyway. Killing people is his passion". I knew it was over, something always goes wrong when you add anyone other than yourself. "Now, we all going down because a mother fucker don't listen. I told y 'all from the jump that if y'all listen to what I say nobody would get dead and we would all get what we wanted. But there's a Jesse James in every bunch! "It might ease your mind to know that no one saw us". I look in amazement. I realize that what could go wrong did. I'm not really worried though because my primary goal was to obtain financial resources for my family and if at all possible, be out of here with them to enjoy it. I look at frank, "I'll make it right, it's not your fault". We go back into the room where everybody is dividing up the spoils. I look at everyone and put on a face of happiness as to keep everyone off guard. "Where's my share, I ask, bag my cut up so I can start livin too"? Tracey pushes me a couple of stacks of money. I place it in a knap sack. "it all good my nigger", Tracey asserts, its all good". Polo looks at me and says, "You the man right now baby. I knew you could make it happen. And with Ronnie under the arm pits we got more of this coming in", pointing to the money and the drugs. Tracey is puffing a joint that almost chokes him to death. 'Word up, you the man. The bodiguas going to be knocking down the doors now. They aint got nobody to push that shit but us". I let him no in so many words that was the least of our problems right now. "Yeah, well, that's another story. Right now, I got some shit to take care of". I walk out the door heading for my house taking the same route back that I took the past two days. I knew as soon as I walked out of the door rob would be curious as to what me and frank was talking about in the back room. he started inquiring as soon as I left. "What did he want to talk to you about", asking frank the question. 'Frank knew what was up. "Oh, nothing big. I told him everything went down smooth and not to worry". "And what did he say when you told him that", rob asked? 'That everything would be alright'. Frank was twisting my words so he would n't cause conflict. Rob ponders what frank says as if he has got something up his sleeve. On the way home, I see none other than my favorite detective. I think he has esp. or something. "Hey Mr. brown, it's me again. I thought you might want to know somebody just knocked off a fixture in the hood. "Why would I want to know that", I asked? 'Because when shit falls, it falls hard. And you know what; the wrong person usually ends up stinking. I'm still watching you, and believe you me, if I watch a little longer; I'm going to get the answers to my problem". He drives off. He and his partner are talking as they drive off. "You ever thought for once that he might not be thinking about any wrong doing", he asks harts field? "Please, he got the mark of the beast now. Once you get that first felony, society says its over, and they respond by committing more crimes. I'd say he was ripened for another murder. Five says he's guilty as sin and im going to prove it". "The bet is sealed, "you're on". I get back to my house and of course, I had to knock on the door. I still don't have a key yet. My sister opens the door. "Mommy just called and asked if you were here". "Did she say what she wanted"? "No, she just wanted to speak to you, I guess". 'Wait ,I have something I want to talk to you about. But first, you have to promise me two things". She looks at me crazy, "what"? "I need your word first". "Yes, you have my word, but if you were not my brother I would never think about promising or giving my oath blindly". I spit it out, "I came across a few dollars and I don't want mommy to know but I want you to look after her with it. It's not a million or nothing like that but it's enough to make it for a good while". I open the bag to show her the contents. "That's more than a few dollars. Where did you get this money? Sha, please, tell me your not on your way back to jail. Did you kill somebody"? I put her mind at ease, even if I wasn't sure what would become of me. 'No, I haven't killed anybody. Just promise me that whatever happens you'll take care of mamma for me. I love you and mamma with all my heart. You know that don't you"? 'Yeah, I know. Sha..., there is a long pause, how come you never told about polo and Tracey being with you that day? You see they never attempted to look out for you". I had to give an answer that was true to myself. "At first I believed they were really my homeboys but as the years went on I saw otherwise. All in all though, there was no need for more than one person to go to jail for the same crime, even if I was duped into doing it. I always felt that was the hand given to me, I could do nothing but play. They too must play with the hands they have been dealt, and sooner or later, they'll be holdin pairs and someone else will have a royal flush. Now go put this in your room". I hand her the bag. She shakes it and kisses me on the forehead. "See you when I get back. I got to go to nanas house in jersey to pick up mommy's dress she borrowed". I go to my room and find my jail bag with my belongings in it. I take out my favorite books that kept me going while I was doing my bid. The prince and the art of war. I wanted to read sections from each to refresh my memory on the proper courses of actions for the situation I was in. I knew I had to kill rob for one; he is such a loose cannon. Killing him will certainly kill the leads. I go downstairs in front of the building to absorb it all and catch some air.

Rob and the rest of them are still at the spot. He is fucked up as hell and begins talking off the wall. They all still over there celebrating. In his drunken stupor, he addresses polo and Tracey. "Your boy was too good to party with us? That mother-fucking fly by night think he can just be in just like that, take our loot? Hell, my motherfucking loot, I do all the killing round this mother fucker". "You roasted man, go home and get some sleep", Tracey demands. "Fuck sleep. I'm gonna sleep when I goddamn feel like sleepin. Polo ordered someone to get Tracey some milk. Rob was not finished with his tirade. "You two niggers always undermining everybody else. We didn't really need your man. I think its time I assumed my position on this ship. I should be the captain". Polo sarcastically concedes. "That's what you want, than you can have it. I'm not trying to be no captain. Everybody is equal. Nobody else is complaining about the decision to bring sha in". Frank tries to break the ice. "Y'all know he don't mean none of this shit he kicken. He's just tore up, that's all". Frank looks at rob. "Come on baby boy, let's go for a walk. I'll go with you to the corner store to get you some coffee and milk". Rob and frank leave for the store. Polo and Tracey are holding a side bar about what just went down. "That nigger is a loose cannon. He goona get all our asses knocked". "Tracey makes light of robs comments. "Aint nobody getting knocked. By tomorrow he's not even going to remember a word he said". "Polo is not convinced, "keep believing that. He already showed us its all about him. He's ego-trippin. They say that when you drunk you must tell the truth. He's telling us exactly how he feels. The sooner we realize that the better". "Well, just wait it out until he comes down, and take it from there. Now, I want to finish partying". He holds up some of the money in his hand. "We got more to be happy about than sad". Rob and frank are in the store across the street. He is trying to sober rob up with milk and coffee. Frank is holding him up." Alright, you gotta stand up for me so I can go to the fridge and get you some milk". He is dragging him around the store. He grabs the milk from the fridge and goes to the counter to pay for it. "Can I get a coffee, black, no sugar", talking to the counter person. He motions to rob. "Here, lean on this". Rob leans on an ice freezer with his hands stretched out over it. Detective hartsfield is on his way in the store to get coffee. Harts field is outside talking to his partner. "I'm going in here to get a donut and some coffee. You want something", asking his partner? He answers, "A bag of chips". Harts field enters the store. He greets the cashier as he enters. "Hey arty, what you no good. Business slow tonight"? Arty responds, "Not since you walked in. how's the misses, she throw you out yet"? "No, not yet". He walks to the counter to pay for the donut. Rob is still leaning over the icebox. Hartsfield notices the watch on robs hand because it is flooded with diamonds. He inquires because he know it is not everyday a man with a watch like the one he is looking for finds its way in his space and time. "Nice watch. What, you struck the lotto? Where'd you buy it? I want to own one just like it someday". Rob is obviously still fucked up. You can tell by his response. "Your mother bought it for me!" frank knows he is in deep shit. It also didn't dawn on him that that was jacks watch or that he had even had it on. All of the excitement about the money made them all blind. "You'll have to excuse him, he's a little tipsy that's all". "You can say that again. Let's see if downtown can take him off his toes and put him on his feet". Hartfield signals for his partner to come to his assistance. Frank tries to squash what he knows will be bad for him and rob if he has to go downtown. "There's no need for that officer. I can get in a cab with him and see that he gets in his house". Hartsfield is not amused and he knows this is an opportunity of a lifetime.

"I bet you can, but just to be on the safe side, I think I better take him in. I couldn't live with myself if he stumbles and busts his head or something". Hartsfield proceeds to handcuff rob to take him to the precinct. They take him downtown and charge him with disorderly conduct as a legal means to hold him in custody. Frank goes back to the spot to let everyone know that rob has just been arrested. He's out of breath from running from the store to the spot. He knocks on the door. "Tracey answers from behind the door, "who is it?" "Me nitty". Tracey opens the door. "They got rob"! Tracey doesn't really know how to respond other than to ask the obvious. "What, who got rob"? Everybody is aroused now, listening intently. " 5-0 got rob. When we was in the store, he was acting up and a knocker was in the store. He took him downtown. He was asking bout a watch that rob had on. I think he took that shit from jack. I didn't even notice it. We got to go get rob out of there before they find out about the watch". Polo is trying to maintain his composer. "Calm down mother fucker. First things first. What watch? I know dam well you aint talking about nothing taken from where we said don't take nothing from". Frank is looking stupid. "I aint know he had it at first". Polo grabs him and throws him against the wall. They know they have to get down to the precinct before this nigger starts acting like a parrot.

11

At the police station rob is coming out of his stupor some-what. Hartsfield is digging for a break through in his case by bombarding rob with tons of questions. "Talk to me you mur-dering mother fucker. Give me what I need to know and you can go in that cell and sleep all day if you want to. I've seen your kind before. I've been on the job a long time." Rob responds, not sure of what he is really saying. "All I know is I didn't kill nobody". That's what hartsfield loves to hear. Go right ahead, open up the door. "What are you implying, you know who did"? "I aint say that, but your boy, good ole Mr. Brown might know something". He doesn't know it but he is getting just the rise out of hartsfield that he has been craving forever and a day. This is a chance of a lifetime to get sha-heem. Hartsfield is looking at his partner so that he can be mindful of the bet they made. "You mean shaheem"? Rob leads him into it. He is obviously getting sober by the minute. "You said it, I didn't. Anyway, you do the math. He already got a murder charge relating to greed and soon as he hits the streets, the same thing happens! Sounds like somebody didn't learn their lesson. " hartsfield is thirsty now. "Come on son. Work with me. You got the watch, you gonna have to come up with a little bit more than that". As hartsfield finishes his sen-tence, rob sees Tracey and polo entering the precinct. "Oh shit!" robs outburst makes harts field turn around. Just as he does, the desk officer points to him to direct Tracey and polo to his desk. Rob is pissing in his pants. "Look, I didn't tell you anything"! Hartsfield doesn't want him to punk out on him now; he's too close to getting his man. "Hold tight. Keep your panties on". Tracey and polo, along with frank, reach harts-fields' desk and look at rob in a suspicious manner. Hartsfield wants to know why do they feel they owe him a visit. "How may I help you boys". Polo, with a look of disdain, "you can help us by letting us know if you chargin our boy with anything so we can meet you at the court house with bail". Hartsfield sees things slippin away from him by the minute. 'Now, now now. Don't go sending "your boy" downtown in front of no judge before his time. You'll all have your turn at that". Tracey gets mad, "and what the fuck that's suppose to mean"? In a smooth tone hartsfield delivers his response, "I'm just callin it like I see it! But anyway, that's a story of its own. I'm not going to hold him. I think he's sobered up rather nicely. As for you future convicts, I suggest you stay the fuck away from Mr. Brown". Tracey is not trying to here the rhetoric "is he free to go now or what"? As he uncuffs him, he lets them know they were free to take him. "Polo just couldn't help himself. He had to get a dig in. "thank you overseer, I mean officer". They are exiting out of the precinct but before they do hartsfield calls to rob. They all turn around. "Hey Robert!" he turns around and harts field winks at him like a bitch would wink at a nigger. "Thanks rob". They all turn back around and exit the precinct. Outside a touch of class is waiting for them. They all get into the joint. Rob is in the middle of the back seat... polo is up front and Tracey is in the drivers seat. Frank is on one side of the door and someone else is on the other. Polo directs his anger at rob. "Seems like you was having a pretty good conversation. I almost didn't want to interrupt. Rob tries to act mad to cloak his deceit. "Fuck you. What I look like a snitch"? Polo shoots right back, "you said it, I didn't". "Who the fuck am I going to snitch on. I'll be hanging my dam self"? Tracey confirms his statement, "I'm glad you know that"! Rob notices that they are driving towards the water. Just as he realizes it, polo puts the automatic lock on the door, locking all four doors. Rob wants answers, "why are we going this way? I know we not going to pick up no work with all of us in here"! Polo looks at Tracey, smiling lightly. "Aint nobody picking up nothing. We going to drop something off".

More questions from rob ensues, "is there work in the car"? Tracey clears that one up, "aint no work in this ride but this joint is dirty as a mother fucker", referring to robs snitching ass. Realizing what's happening rob gets frantic. "I know y'all don't think I told. Oh, it's like that. That's how y'all mother fuckers going out"? Rob reaches for the door. There is a police car behind them. From Tracey's rear view mirror, he spots the police car. He calmly looks over at polo. " 5-0 right behind us. Polo looks in the rear view mirror. He turns on the music, cracks the window slightly and tells everyone to make movements to the rhythm of the beat. Polo gives instructions, "just start singing and clapping to the song". The cops move to the side of the car while the light is still red. Rob is trying to get some line of communication to the cops, but the sound of the music and everybody singing is drowning him out. The police officer looks across at Tracey and signals him to roll the window down, which he does. "Have fun but turn it down some". Tracey gives the officer a thumbs up, "thanks officer". The police car drives off. The officer looks at his partner. "Their way too noisy to be guilty of anything" his partner replies, "you know how they are when they hear that dam rap music. Its like monkeys going on a banana hunt". Back in the touch of class, Tracey has an expression of relief on his face. They reach the Westside under the one train where the water is. They all get out of the car. Tracey reaches under the seat to get his joint. Polo releases the trunk lock and Tracey recovers the other pistol. Rob, realizing this is his last chance to save his life. "Yo, frank, you my nigger. You going to let these niggers fade me"? Frank knows his hands are tied and has no problem letting him no it. "I wash my hands. You out of control now. You don't listen to nobody". Polo wants him to know the real deal. "I'm not going to fade you. You gonna fade you. I'm going to give you a chance to run like hell". Rob knows there is a catch. "And than what"? "And than nothing, that's it" "if you was going to let me run, why you brought me over here than"? "Because this is your track". He lifts his hands toward the Hudson River indicating that was the track he was talking about. "You could either sink or swim. At least you have a chance at life". Rob looks at the water and than comes to a resolve about his fate. "Alright than. If this is how it s got to be". He grabs frank and falls down backwards into the river, taking frank with him. "We'll see you in hell nigger". Tracey tries to grab frank but he is unsuccessful. Frank manages to hold onto a log at the base of the dock. The undercurrent is dragging rob under and he's trying to hold on to frank, which in essence, is pulling frank off the log. Frank is crying for help, "somebody help me! Please help me"! Tracey sees a long piece of railing pipe about six feet away. He grabs it and puts it in the water to assist frank. Polo sees that frank has a chance of survival and takes the pole away from Tracey, pretending to help. "Here gimme" taking the poll from Tracey. He yells down to frank. "Grab it with both hands". Frank lets go of the log and tries to grab the pole with both hands. Polo pushes the pole into franks face and than let's the pole go. He tries to make it appear as if he did it by accident but Tracey is not convinced. 'What the fuck did you just do? You buggin yo! I saw what you just did and don't say I'm trippin because I aint smoke shit today"! Polo doesn't even acknowledge what he said, "let's get the fuck outta here. We can talk about this later. Unless of course you wanna get knocked"! Tracey wants answers, "naw, fuck that, lets discuss this shit now. How you livin"? "Look, we just killed two birds with one stone. Now there's nobody that can come between our peace, freedom and money. Except for this nigger right here"! He points his gun at the other guy that was with them, who was also with frank and rob when fats was killed. He shoots him two times in the chest and he drops to the floor. Tracey is beginning to numb towards it. "You're sick you know that"? Polo ignores him and focuses on the situation at hand," come on, grab his legs. Help me dump the mother fucker". Tracey grabs his legs hesitantly and they walk over to the railing, lift the body up and throw him over. They both have blood on their jackets. Polo takes both jackets and puts them in the garbage can. "Give me your jacket", polo demands. Tracey hands it to him. After throwing them in the dumpster, polo walks over to the car. "You just gonna leave them", Tracey asks? Polo gets a bottle of alcohol out of the trunk. "Shut up. Do I look like I got stupid printed on my forehead"? He pours the alcohol on the jackets and sets them on fire. "Let's get the fuck out of here"! They get into the car and drive off. As they are driving polo spots, a sanitation truck and sanitation man picking up garbage. Polo takes the paper bag from the glove compartment, wipes off the gun with the handkerchief, places the gun in the bag, get out and throws the bag in the back of the sanitation truck. Polo gets the sanitation mans attention, "no need putting it in the garbage can when you just emptied it". The sanitation man responds in kind, "yeah right, thanks for helping keep New York clean"! Polo looks at him and jumps back into the car. They head back to the spot.

12

I go to the spot to look for rob. I walk up the stairs, knock on the door. There is someone in front of the door purchasing work. The money and the drugs are exchanged through the hole in the door. "Yeah what's up"? "Let me get two of them things". 'Slip the money through". The buyer slides the money through. He slides the buyer two bags of dope. I am right behind him but the nigger behind the door doesn't realize that it's me standing there. "Yeah, next. How may you want"? "It's me sha". He opens the door and lets me in. not wasting anytime he gives me the run down. " aint nobody here. They all went to the precinct to get rob". 'for what" I said? "He was on the tipsy side a little while ago so him and frank went down to the A-rabs to get some milk to calm his ass down. Next thing I know, frank came in here all out of breath and shit talking about rob was arrested". I get irate. 'I knew that mother fucker was a weak link. The moment I saw him putting those bullets in that clip with his bare hands. But I tell you what, that fool going down by his dam self! I aint payin for nobody else's mistake no more". We are interrupted by a knock on the door. Its Tracey and polo. The hustler walks over to the peephole, looks through it and opens the door. "It lets me know who it is before he opened the door. "Its polo and T". Polo, concerned about paper, 'you finished that pack yet", to the hustler. "Naw, I got half a pack left". "Cool". He is looking at me and he notices an air of uneasiness. "What you looking all lit up for my nigger"? "You know what for, your loose ass homeboy, that's what for. Where he at anyway"? Polo can't wait to get it out. "Who, rob? Yo sha, trust me, you or nobody else gotta worry about that nigger dropping dimes on nobody. It's all good; he is sleeping with the fishes". "I hope its all good, I'm tired of doing time. "Get your mind off of that time shit. Aint none of us doing no time. Matter of fact... lets close this shit up and go to Nells. We going to celebrate peace, freedom, and money".

When we got to the club, nightfall was hitting the city already. No one bothered to change their clothes because polo and Tracey had juice at the club. They could come dressed anyway they wanted. Outside there is a big neon sign that says, "Nells joint". There are players and bitches standing outside dressed in haberdasher wear. The young hustler from the spot is the driver. He brings the car to a complete stop than gets out to open the back doors to let everyone out as if he was a chauffeur or something. We are all dressed in thug shit, not to mention what I am dressed in. we are noticeable just because of that fact alone. We are ushered in by two bouncer niggers that polo just slipped three crisp hundred-dollar bills to. We get to the middle of the dance floor were we are greeted by the owner. It is Nell; she is a big-breasted woman with tits as beautiful as a cassava Mellon. She puts her breasts in polo's' face, you can tell that is her customary greeting to niggers she knows. "Boy, if I didn't have a crush on your little ass I'd kick your behind outta here. My customers not gonna believe shit stink if I keep letting y'all come in like this. You know what type of joint I run, and don't say you don't look right in dress up clothes cause I saw you in a suit at Al B's funeral last month". He kisses her on the cheek to butter her up a bit. "You got it, you got it. Next time we come in here we going to be correct". She points her finger at him in a joking manner, "I'm not playing, I mean it now". As the last word is uttered, she is whisked away to the dance floor by one of the people in the bar. Tracey and me are just caught up in the atmosphere. I am being observant. Anywhere there is a lot of niggers I want to keep my eyes and ears open. Polo raises his voice above the music so that we could make out what he was trying to say. "I don't know about y'all but I'm about to get my drink on". Polo leaves us and starts to mingle his way to the bar. A couple of seconds later, Tracey leaves me standing there and gets whisked to the dance floor by some hoochie. On the other side of town, the police are on the scene of the crime by the Westside highway. A fisherman saw the bodies of frank and rob floating in the Hudson and called the police. Two detectives are standing over the bodies that are covered with two white sheets. Yellow tape is surrounding the area where the bodies are. One detective is smoking a cigar. While the two detectives are standing over the bodies talking, harts field and his partner drive up. They seem to have homicide locked in this naked city. The detective smoking the cigar recognizes harts field as he is getting out of his car. Detective Noble sees who it is and throws his cigar to the ground, "aw, fuck"! Motioning in the direction of his partner, detective lang. "if it isn't the two super crime fighters themselves"! harts field is in a somewhat playful mood so he goes along. "You got a lot of jokes lang. what are you, a comedian now? You haven't solved a case I years". Lang gets serious, "fuck you"! Noble gets serious and inquires as to what he owes their presence. "What brings the both of yous over this side of town anyway"? harts field has a slick reply. "Well see, that's why were super cops. Unlike you guys, we know what's going on. The 2-6 and the 2-8 get the Westside highway. Like it or not, it's a we thing on this one. So whatta weeee got"? Noble doesn't even bother to complain, he knows he could use the help. "We got two shits who decided to take a dip in unfamiliar waters". Harts field pulls the sheet back off the bodies and immediately recognizes both bodies. He looks at his partner while holding the sheet up and they both give off a look of disbelief and familiarity. "Looks like these two stiffs belong to me", harts field asserts. Lang is confused. "What"? "Yea, you heard what I said. You got a one frank white, aka frank nitty, and Robert Packwood, aka, murder rob. Both east side, small time thugsters. Last seen at the station house a couple of hours ago. I was questioning ol Robert here..." "He lifts the sheet over robs head again as if to take one more look. " I was questioning him about the shooting death of fat jack. When I was done, frank and his other associates came to get his half drunk ass". Harts field partner once to get in on the humor. "Well, now that we've identified our Olympic swimmers, I guess we can work on solving this thing. Who was the first on the scene"? It was a rookie. He blurts out to harts fields partner, "me and my partner sir". Harts field partner look at the uniformed officer in anticipation of more information. Me and my partner sir is just not enough to work with. "Well that's it? Me and my part-ner sir! Where's the witness, if there is one. Who called it in"? The rookie looks in shock as if he didn't think he was expect-ed to know all of that. "Oh, he's over there. A fisherman spot-ted them". hartsfield partner looks over in the direction that the rookie pointed and sees the fisherman talking to another uniformed cop. He and hartsfield go over to interrogate the fisherman. While they walk over, harts field says, "As dumb as these rookies are, you would think they manufactured them on an assembly line". His partner laughs. They approach the witness. "Hello sir', his partner Davis says. He extends his hands to shake the fishersman hands.

My name is detective Davis and this is my partner, detec-tive hartsfield. You mind if we ask you a few questions"? "Of course I mind, but since I called it in I guess I opened the door for questioning now didn't I"? "I guess you did" Davis says, how did you discover the body"? "Like I said when I called it in, they were floating out there like two fish begging to be hooked, lined and sinked". Harts field once to clear his per-sonal suspicions. Everyone's a suspect in his mind. "You nor-mally fish in the Hudson"? Excitedly the fisherman responds. "Shit yea. As dirty as this water is, they beg for you to catch em. Hell, I just do it for the sport of it anyway. I'm retired you know"! "Did you

see anything unusual out here today, any strange people around"? "What's not unusual in New York? Look, I can't help anymore than I have. I aint seen nothing else but those two bodies". Davis is satisfied. "Okay sir. Thanks for your help. Try not to catch anymore big fish out here". The fisherman is not amused by the joke. "Yeah right". Davis and harts field walk to their car, conversing along the way. "So what do you think", hartsfield asks Davis. "Think about what, that guy? His story is legitimate" "no, not that guy. Mr. Brown, that guy, that's who"? Davis opens the door of the car, gets in and opens hart fields door from the inside by pulling the latch up. Hartsfield finishes his spiel. "Think about it, everything points to him. All this shit started when he hits the street". "Does that make him guilty of two double murders? Besides, both of your boys back there left the precinct with those two gang bangers from Fifth Avenue". "Who, polo and Tracey? Shit, they may run a little dope out of 32nd street but they aint doin no killing. But for the sake of an argument, go to 32nd. Let's see what they know".

14

Back at the club, I am in the bathroom on the toilet. There are sinks lined in a row and each sink has a big mirror with lights all around it. Ronnie, the drug dealer we robbed enters the bathroom to piss and fix himself up. As I slightly open the door of the toilet stall, I see Ronnie. I close the door back and lock it. I pull out my joint, which was in my shoe when I came in. Ronnie's partner comes ion shortly after and they began conversation the bathroom. I can hear them loud and clear. " I still don't know how you going to get them to front you for four of them things when you haven't paid for the other three you got on consignment". Ronnie's not pressed and it shows. He sounds as if he has it all figured out. "Don't worry about it. I got everything covered. Now go back out there and keep those mother fuckers laughing". Ronnie's partner exits back to the table where he and Ronnie were discussing business with the bodiguas. I wait for a guy to finish pissing to exit the bathroom so I can rap to Ronnie. I open the stall door and points my pistol at Ronnie. Ronnie sees me in the mirror but it is far too late to make any sudden move. He knows I got the drop on him. "Ah, shit. It hasn't even been a week yet"! I poke him in the side with the nose of the gun. "Chill out, I'm not here to get anything from you. In fact, I'm here to offer you something. You see, I got a proposition that you can't refuse". Ronnie looks like, what kind of proposition you got for me. "Oh yea, what"? "How would you like half of your money back, and the other thing squashed? I'll even give up the neg-atives, referring to the pictures". "Is this a trick question or what"? I open the bathroom door slightly and instruct him to look outside. "Look out on the dance floor and tell me what you see". He looks out, but doesn't see what I wanted him to see at first glance. "I see people dancing". "What else do you see"? He looks again. "What you want me to see"? "Look over to your far left". It is Tracey and polo dancing next to each other. They are both semi drunk. Ronnie finally sees what he wants him to see. "It's your partners". "They were my partners until they crossed me some time ago. Now its time for peter to pay Paul and your going to help them pay it". "Why should I help you"? "The same reason I shouldn't paste those photos on every corner, mutual interest. Now, I want you to go out there, cause a commotion, and as everybody gets to trampling for the door, bang, bang, you hit them. After that, you just run out with everybody else and it's all good". "What about my money"? "Just to let you know, I'm not shiesty, I'll bring the loot to your crib". 'And the pictures"? 'The pictures too. Now take care of that". Ronnie exits the bathroom and goes back to the table with his partner and connect. He is still unnoticed by Tracey and polo. After he shares a few words with the people at his table, his partner gets up and goes over to the Deejay. He turns off the music and fires two shots up into the air. It is now chaotic but Ronnie has his eyes fixed on polo and Tracey all the while. Ronnie walks calmly in the midst of all the chaos and pumps two in each of their chests. He gets to about three feet away from them. They are oblivious. 'Choke on this mother fuckers"! Polo tries to reach but he hits him in the chest before he can even touch his gun. He than hits Tracey almost in the same motion. He than stashes the gun in his waist and runs out with the crowd. I am at the bathroom door standing there watching everything as it unfolded. There is still commotion but I am very much in control of myself. While that is going on Davis and harts field gets the call over their radios that shots have been fired at Nells. Their dipping and dodging traffic to get here. When things start to settle a bit, I go out from the sanutary of the bathroom corridor. I can see polo is still alive. He is bleeding from the mouth and chest. I go over to him and put my arms around him as if to console him. He is looking up at me, his eyes looking like he is fading away towards the light. He says in a low voice, "I'm going to die man, I'm going to die"! I started to cry crocodile tears; I had to make it look as authentic as possible. "Naw, you, you gonna make it. Who did this to you"? I hear police sirens in the distance and realize it was time to do the do. I hold my thumb and forefinger on polo's' nostrils and cover his mouth with my other hand. Polo starts to choke on his own blood and dies with his eyes open, looking up at me. I close his eyes to keep from having to look at him. "Wherever going, I hope you don't cross nobody there". I take some of the blood on polo's mouth and blood soaked shirt and begin to smear it on my face and shirt. Harts field and Davis enter, along with several other uniformed officers. Immediately I go into this big hysterical act. Harts field has had enough." So you really did it, Mr. Brown". I am sobbing, not paying him any mind, as to be caught up in the moment. "Did what? Now is not the time for you to be fucking with me"! harts field grabs me. "Oh no, haven't begun to fuck with you. I always knew you were a ruthless low life scum, but this is the bottom of the barrel…. , he looks at the bodies, even for you". "Get the fuck off of me', I urge. Davis grabs him off of me. "Get a hold of yourself. What, you want to lose your job"? Chide in, "yeah, that's what he wants. You have been fucking with me ever since I hit these streets. Tryin to pin one thing on me after the other. And to add insult to injury, you accuse me of doing the unthinkable to the two niggers that were raised like my brothers. But you know what, it won't work. Everybody that was in this joint and they mamma know I don't know what the fuck is going on". Harts field is no moved one bit by the story. "You got them all fooled, the parole board, the community, and your poor ole mother"> harts field looks at Davis. "You even got my partner fooled. But me, oh no, not me. Not for one minute. I know your kind. You aint shit. You might not get yours now, but sooner or later it'll all catch up to you". 'And you know what, maybe you're right. If I am doing anything displeasing to the man upstairs I will pay for it.

But it won't be by your hands, and it certainly won't be by your wit. Now if im not being charged with anything, and I know I'm not, I'm going to go home and give myself some quiet time. I just lost two friends'. I get up and start walking towards the exit with my back to them. Davis looks at harts field and says, "I guess this means you're not going to take him down to the station for questioning"? "what, and waste my time/ he's probably got a lie so tight you can't stick a needle through it'.

15

I exit and head straight for the spot to go and get the rest of the money that polo and Tracey had their. I also get the copies of the pictures of Ronnie. I go to the all night post office on the deuce and mail the pictures of Ronnie to detective harts field. I mail the money next day service to my mother. I have two identical bags with me. One has the money in it and the other has socks and underwear. I call Ronnie and tell him to meet me on 125th street, at the train station by mc Donald's in fifteen minutes. "Hello, Ron" he picks up. "Yeah, who this"? "That nigger that's about to change your life. Meet me on 125th street by the one train in fifteen minutes, and come alone. "You told me that you would meet me here'. "Change of plans. Fifteen minutes". I hang up. I arrive at the train station. Ronnie is already there. We are both somewhat nervous. The train is about to reach the station. Ronnie is looking around. "So, you got that for me"? 'all in the bag and accounted for". "Well give it here". I pass him a bag. "Thanks, nice doing business with you. Now I have something for you." He shoots me twice in the upper area. The gun has a silencer on it. I drop to the floor and Ronnie gets on the train and takes off. I am lying in a pool of blood. I can feel the life slipping away from me. Someone must have called 911 because I can hear ambulances coming. I hear them but I don't see them. I knew this would happen. There is no honor among thieves. I had a back up plan anyway. Ronnie has to be sick opening that bag to find nothing more than a bunch of smelly socks and underwear. I of course recovered, after being in the hospital for nearly six months. It left me partly paralyzed on my right side. I have not seen my mother and I doubt I ever will again. She needs to live in peace and so do I. I have enough loot to keep it moving, and that is what I am going to do. I never had any friends after that, shit I never had any in the first place. Its a thousand stories in the naked city. This is my story and I am sticking to it.

Dedications

This book is dedicated to the niggers in the hood who no one believes will ever amount to anything. It is for the niggers that have done hard time and see the benefits of being free. This is for all the niggers who have to put up with shit they don't want to put up with just so they can make it right. this is for the killers who know what it feels like to take a niggers life, only to have some young punk disrespect you on the street, knowing full well that if this was another place and time you would have left him dead and stinking. This is for the fatherless child who grew up with parents that didn't give a fuck about him or her. This is for the bastard child and the child who's father was absent in their lives because mamma couldn't get along with daddy or he was serving more time than a little bit. This is for the whores who have loss their dignity and feel they can't regain it back. Your priceless ladies. This is for the three time felon who bites his tongue everyday to keep from knocking his girl head clean off her face because he know s the next felony puts his lights out. This is for the man that has played daddy to his girl's kids only to be disrespected. This is to the niggers on lock down who will never get the opportunity to have a second chance at making it right. This is to the one thing that has ever meant anything to me. This is to the many men and women who have been falsely convicted of a crime they didn't commit and the D.A. knows it but just wanted a body. This is to the niggers that have dreams but don't know how to execute those dreams. This is for the fake friends who still have the opportunity to make it right with the niggers they crossed. This is for the street hustler that cant tell you what 25% of 100 is but can tell you how to put a quarter of cut on every ounce of dope he mixes. You're a mathematician in your own way. This is for all the real men I know that will curse a three hundred pound nigger out the same way he would curse a nigger out that weighs ninety pounds soaking wet. A real man is impartial. This is for all my niggers that don't talk about what they would have done to a nigger but rather do what they wanted to have done to a nigger. Real people do real things. This is for my niggers that would rather risk life, limb and freedom to put food on the table for their lobed ones, only god can judge you. This is for the nigger that comes home from jail with no family or friends and is still expected to make it on his own. This is for the niggerswho had vision and had to put up with a bitches shit, even when you felt like they were beneath you. This is not for you fake ass rappers who live other niggers lives in your raps and try to give the public the impression that you lived that type of lifestyle when you know in your heart your own community see you ass suckers. This is not for the phony rappers who get highlighted on VH1, before htye were stars, and cribs. More specifically, Nelly, you was no baller. Between you and the st. lunatics, ya'll could only get a thousand dollars up to put your music out. Real hustlers have more than a thousand dollars in their possession. You're just a bubble gum rapper that I would be fucking in jail. Jah-rule, I saw you rapping for food on their MTV special they did on you. You guys should know they got old footage on your that conflicts with what you niggers tell the public. You was defiantly a bum. Damon dash, I've lived in Harlem all my life, getting money I might add. Nobody knew you until roca fella. Ask your man Terrell Mackey about me. Puff daddy, you not even from Harlem. Why don't you shout out Mount Vernon and stop being ashamed of being from there? Being from Harlem doesn't make you a man. Irv gotti, change your name back. Master P, you got that money to get on from your grandfather, not hustling. That tells me that you were starving before that. Ten thousand is not much, shit I had that in my pocket as a teenager. Jermaine Dupree, you was a clown ass dancer. You little crooked teeth jigga boo. Real niggers are serious, they don't clown and buffoon for money, at no expense. If your over twenty one you shouldn't be rapping anyway. Grow up and leave that shit for your children. Real men don't rap, that's why your girls don't have no respect for you now. You want to run around stages like your fifteen or something. Freeway and beanie Mack, or big Mack, whatever your name is. Nothing about either one of you says baller. Even with rap money, now you niggers wouldn't know what class is if it hit you in the face? Go climb back into your ugly mamma womb. All you niggers with gold teeth in your mouth, that aint cool either. I don't care if you do got millions. Balers don't put that shit in their mouth. I wouldn't eat out with none of you stink breath niggers. That shit is embarrassing, not to mention that shit played out in the eighties. It also says southern low life nigger.

Gutter Publications
1461 a 1st ave ste 234
New York, NY 10021
guttermag.com
914-476-9686